MASTERED BY DEGREES

THE COLLECTION

SELENA POWERS

CYPRESS PRESS, LLC

Title: MASTERED BY DEGREES: THE COLLECTION / Selena Powers
Description: Paperback First Edition
Publication Date: September 21st, 2023
Cover Design: Selena Powers
Formatting: Samantha Moran, Obsidian Inkwell Publishing, LLC

Paperback ISBN-13: 979-8-9860399-3-0
Also available as an ebook edition.

ABOUT THE PURCHASE OF THIS BOOK

CONTENTS

INITIATION

BOOK ONE

MASTERED BY DEGREES

Initiation

BUTTERFLY
CHAPTER ONE

I t's hard watching other people in love.

PDA doesn't bother me. I'm twenty-four, not seventy-four. And I'm not a prude. Well, at least I wouldn't be if given the chance. I have fantasies. I can be naughty. I think. I guess that's the real problem. There's not been much of an opportunity to explore those fantasies, to be on the receiving end of PDA.

But having a front row seat to what you imagine real love looks like...

...the smiles...

...the touches...

...the looks...

That's like knowing the winning numbers to the lottery but getting to the counter too late to buy a ticket.

My uber hot roommate, Lily, and her equally hot boyfriend, Jon, and I are ridesharing to the French Quarter for an afternoon of shopping. Ok. They will be shopping. I will be window shopping. I haven't waited four years for my inheritance to come through to waste it on brand name clothes and shoes that would see nothing but the inside of my closet.

Jon and Lily are the main floor attraction in the PDA lovefest. To be fair, it's pretty tame. No loud lip smacking or roving hands thank god. Just her head on his shoulder. His thumb making casual little circles on the inside of her wrist.

"I can't believe you're not at the library on a Tuesday afternoon, Bree." Lily uncrossed and crossed her long legs, our thighs meeting hip to knee even in the spacious confines of the Lincoln Towncar she'd ordered for our ride. "A butterfly somewhere must be flapping its wings pretty hard for this to happen."

I sink further into the corner of the Towncar as tingles of awareness touch places I'd sooner not think about where Lily is concerned. "I always schedule a sick day on the thirty-sixth Tuesday of the year."

The driver smothers a laugh behind a cough. Lily and Jon join in.

"What?" I hold my hands out, trying to grab a whiff of dignity from the air. I know they are joking, but still... "I want to graduate early if possible. I've waited long enough to get my life started."

Most people my age already have their degree. My love life isn't the only area where I am a late bloomer. Lily is a few years older, but she's in graduate school. A PhD in economics. Yes, she's beautiful and brilliant. It would be easy to hate her if she wasn't so nice.

The age thing is why the housing gods put me and Lily together in the adult student housing. Older birds of a feather and all that, but she is more the silver breasted broadbill - beautiful, graceful - and I'm the common sparrow.

Who really notices a sparrow?

"Where do you want to be let out, Miss Nguyen?" The driver's piercing eyes find mine in the rear-view mirror but I figure he's just checking traffic and my reflection got in the way.

Rideshare driver is obviously a side gig for him. He has to be a model. One of those guys that stands half-dressed on a beach and advertises something no one recalls after the commercial is over. Or maybe a dancer down in that new club in the Quarter. The Velvet Something. I've heard stories about that place but it's not like I'll ever check them out. I'm not a place-with-stories-for-a-date kind of girl. Not that I've had any dates recently to know.

Lily leans forward, the hem of her purple t-shirt riding high enough in the back to show off the two kitten tattoos on her left hip. "Near the Saenger is fine, Jacob. We can walk from there. Thank you."

As Jacob pulls the car over, I grab my wallet. "How much do I owe you for the ride, Lily?" The potential cost of a Towncar, even divided by three, scares me a little. I'd have taken the bus but when Lily heard my plans for the day and invited me to join her and Jon on the ride downtown, it seemed rude to say no. Guess it will be Ramen for lunch and dinner next week. I shimmy a little against her hips. So worth it.

Lily waves her hand. "Don't worry about it. My mom had a gift certificate from one of her raffles and gave it to me. We have the car for the day."

Jon pulls Lily back against his broad chest. He fills his side of the back seat, all shoulders and biceps. "We're going to grab a bit to eat at Galatoire's. Want to join us?"

I know the place. Fancy. Expensive. And closed on a Tuesday. "I didn't think they were open today."

Jon brushes Lily's hair behind her ear and nuzzles her temple with fish lips until she grins. "My dad goes way back with the owner," he says around his own laugh. "It's just a casual thing. You're more than welcome to come."

He seems sincere and I wouldn't mind having some company today. But the little insecurities of being a third wheel pop up and wobble around my insides.

"No, thanks." I say, but it's reluctant. "Three's a crowd."

"Or a great evening." The delicious smile that accompanies Jon's comment chases a shiver down my spine until is swirls between my legs.

A bloom of heat rises up my neck and I'm sure my cheeks are this embarrassing shade of pink now. "I...I think I'll just head down to the square. I brought my camera and want to take some pictures while the light is still good."

It's as good an excuse as any but I wonder if it sounds as hollow as it feels.

"Too bad. We'd like to have you for lunch."

Lily elbows him in the ribs as she reaches over the front seat for the business card Jacob is already holding out. "Just call this number when you're done, and Jacob will pick you up and take you back to school or wherever you want to go. He's yours for the day."

Mine. If only...

"It'll be my pleasure, Ms. Ngyuen." Those eyes find mine again, only this time there is no rear-view mirror as a buffer. Jacob is giving me some serious eye contact. "Ms. Fontenot. I look forward to picking you up later."

He says my name in a familiar mispronunciation. Fun-to-know. Only when I was growing up, the kids always added a hearty "NOT" at the end. Jacob smiles. A smirk really. I don't know what to do with that.

Luckily Lily clears her throat and snatches me back to

reality. We exit the car and watch Jacob ease back into traffic on Canal as smoothly as he'd tossed out that line.

"Uhh..." Speaking. Words. Wow. A hot guy smiles at me and my brain freezes. "No. You and Jon should use the car. I can take the bus."

Jon wraps his arms around Lily from behind, laying his chin on her shoulder. As tall as he is, he nearly has to fold himself in half but he doesn't look like he minds. "My place is not too far from here. We'll stay there tonight. Let you have the room to yourself."

I spend more time in my shared room alone than I do with my roommate. I always wondered why she bothered to even pay for housing.

"OK." I take the card from Lily, offering her a grateful smile. While my life hadn't been a Dickens novel, even small kindnesses leave me feeling overwhelmed. "That's... I...thank you." I breathe slowly past the lump in my throat. "Please tell your mother I said thank you as well."

"Enjoy the afternoon, Bree." Lily gives me a quick one arm hug, pressing her cheek to mine. Her skin is soft and warm, a spark of kindness against the dry husk of my soul. In my ear, she whispers, "You deserve it."

Jon winks at me, then salutes as he and Lily turn and join hands. "Don't be too good, Bree. It's the French Quarter. Laissez bon temps roule!" His French is perfect.

The two of them move lazily into the foot traffic on North Rampart and it's hard to pull my eyes away. It's more than the great view. Lily walks like she owns the air around her, as if it never occurs to her to doubt her place in the universe. Jon paves the way with his size and easy good looks. Women stop to stare, mouths open, cheeks high with color when he met their gazes. Other men wouldn't dare cross him.

What I wouldn't give to have a little of that in my life. The easy confidence. The willing protector. Love. I am on my own and nothing brings that home each night more than the emptiness of a shared apartment.

"Enough." I say aloud. No one looks at me funny. It's New Orleans after all. People expect a little crazy.

I blend into the mostly tourist traffic along Canal. Late September is a quiet time in terms of people in the city. Mardi Gras is a faded memory. The summer heat is waning but not yet gone. Hurricane season is coming to a close and the storms aren't likely to pop up and ruin a weekend.

I stop at Canal Place, roam the shops for a while. There's a great little lingerie place I drool over every time I'm down here. The stuff is way over my budget even for a splurge but they are having a massive sale and with a little encouragement from the flirty sales clerk, I pick up a satin teddy. Who knows. Maybe it'll even get worn for someone other than me one day.

It's easy to lose time in the French Quarter. The galleries alone can eat up hours. Fresh, hot beignets on the steps of the St. Louis Cathedral, watching the dancers and comedians perform. Tarot readers who'll answer questions about your future career or love life. I can answer at least one of those without divine guidance. Street artists looking to capture the happy couples or happy families on a sixteen by twenty piece of paper. That part of my life would fit on a postcard.

Enough of that. Aunt Katie may have been a bitch unsuitable to raising children, but she is right about that. Whining never gets you anywhere.

Putting a swish in my step – I can pretend confidence if not live it - I head toward my favorite little bar, The Last Glass, for a cocktail, calling Jacob and asking him to pick me up at the Saenger in an hour. The bar is mostly empty on a late Tuesday afternoon. It's even too early for the early evening crowd so I enjoy the quiet and the jukebox and the cocktail then leave to meet Jacob. I'm a little early but won't mind waiting.

As it turns out, I don't have to wait. Jacob is there, leaning against the front end of the dark car, long, long legs stretched out in front and crossed at the ankles. If a man can radiate sex appeal, his neon sign is humming brightly.

He's engrossed in a book, something weighty from the looks of page count. The tie is loose around his neck and the wind has ruffled the dark waves of his hair. It's five o'clock based on the thick stubble showing every ridge and flex of a very square jaw.

Is it wrong to enjoy the view this much? But he is putting it on display. And I did come downtown to window shop.

A noise behind me draws his eyes up and a smile lifts one corner of a mouth made for smiling.

"Miss Fontenot." He drops the book on the hood of the car and those long legs devour the sidewalk between us. He takes the single tiny bag from the lingerie shop. "How was your day?"

Again, I lose the power of speech. I. am. Such. A. Loser. I nod, manage a grunt that sounds like uh-huh. Jacob laughs but it shines in his eyes like amusement, not pity.

"Good." He opens the car door and holds my hand while I step inside, then hands me the lingerie bag. Our fingertips brush. His nails are neat but you can tell the calluses are hard earned. "There's a couple of Cheerwine sodas in the cooler."

My eyes widen. Those are my favorite but they're

impossible to find in the New Orleans area. How did he know?

"And the center console has some snacks if you're hungry. The trip back will take a little while with traffic, so please relax."

I'm digging through the bags of cashews – another favorite – and look up to find Jacob opening an icy can of soda and handing it to me with a napkin around the base.

"Enjoy." He adds a wink then settles back behind the wheel while I try and wipe the drool from the corner of my mouth.

Traffic is as bad as I expect for downtown. Everyone is trying to get home at the same time. Everyone is in a hurry. With the possible exception of me. I like watching Jacob. He's mouthing the words to a song only he can hear and I'm curious what music makes those perfect lips move like that.

"What song has you tapping your fingers?"

Without moving his head, he meets my eyes in the rearview mirror. I can see the right corner of his mouth lift. "Everlast. We're All Gonna Die."

My laugh catches me by surprise and a few clicks on my phone has the bluesy rock rhythm filling the car.

"I knew you had good taste." Jacob is quiet for a moment while he merges onto the interstate. "I went to see them a few years back in New York. The show was –" He mimes and explosion with his fingers.

We fill the next forty minutes easily with talk of music and life. He's getting a business degree. Thinks my science degree is cool. He likes girls with glasses. I wish I was wearing mine.

When we pull up in front of the dorm I'm disappointed to be leaving. I think about asking him out but talk myself out of that idea in the same breath I have it. He's gorgeous. I'm a sparrow.

I go to reach for the door but he cautions me to wait as he shifts into park, then jumps out and comes to open my door. I get the reverse treatment onto the sidewalk.

"Here." I fumble with my purse. "I'd like to give you a tip."

"Ah," Jacob does a half bow, real gallant. "Thank you, Miss Fontenot. My services have been paid for this evening." That wink again. I might have come a little. Damn. "But I appreciate the gesture."

He walks me to the door and opens it, gesturing me inside. "You have a wonderful evening. Maybe we'll see each other again someday."

I sigh. Doubtful. But a girl can dream.

EXPOSED
CHAPTER TWO

S aturday night.

The dorm is quiet tonight. Hell, the whole campus is quiet. Date night. Party night. You name it, it happens on Saturday night.

Unless you're me.

Saturday is study night, like every other night. It's hard enough being a college student that's four years older than the other students in my year. I'm also an introvert.

I prefer the company of a good book or movie, something romantic where the nerdy girl wins the heart of the hot roommate or someone like the hot RideShare driver she thinks might be secretly flirting with her.

Yeah, fiction is great.

My lack of a life meant I had the place to myself. Saturday is my favorite night of the week regardless. Lily and Jon were once again spending the night at his place near the French Quarter. The showers are free. The washing machines are available. Pizza delivery is practically guaranteed within twenty minutes.

OK. It's boring.

After four years of living on Ramen noodles and Jello while my aunt and uncle tied up my parents' estate in probate court, I wasn't going to waste a nickel on expensive clubs and pricey drinks. I was on my own.

Finally.

Despite the loneliness that conjures, I remind myself of what I left behind. Besides, sometimes being alone is a good thing.

Like now.

I light the circle of candles around the room, turn out the thrift store lamps and crawl into bed wearing the satin teddy number I'd bought on sale earlier in the week. Alcohol and twelve deep on the dance floor? Eh. Silky lingerie? Oh yes.

I'm not cheap but I can be bought.

It's something I think Lily would wear. Red. No, *crimson*. The sales lady said it complimented my auburn hair and green eyes. If it had been anyone else standing there, I would have said she was coming on to me. But it was me, after all. And neither men nor women usually noticed me much.

I'm not hideous or anything. I am the Switzerland of sex, however. Neutral.

Most of the time I don't mind.

Tonight, however, I don't worry about that. The teddy does some magic to my body. Maybe it affected my mind because nerve endings are firing to life, crackling beneath the surface of skin warmed by naughty fantasies. The cool silk caresses my nipples, making them pucker and rise against the wispy slip of material.

The lacy bottom slides between my legs, stroking my

pussy like the lovers I dream of at night. Lately the trio of fantasy lovers has my mind in overdrive. My sex aches and tightens at the images. Honeyed skin and eyes of obsidian. Or maybe tall with broad shoulders and a French accent. Piercing eyes, a wink and a smirk.

The face hovers behind the shadows but I don't fill in the blanks too much. Fantasizing about your roommate - or her boyfriend - never turns out well.

I need release, need to spiral away from the ache and into the satisfaction of a healthy orgasm. I'm alone, I push the covers down and let my hand wander across my breasts, pressing the soft material of the teddy firmly against the hard peaks.

I drift into the fantasies I want to play out. When I'm alone. When I'm safe. Dark fantasies. Fantasies that push me to the edge of my safety zone then catch me when I begin to fall.

The lacy thong pulls and presses between my legs, rubbing against the valley of my sex, now wet and warm. The first touch as I slip one finger inside sends shivers radiating to my toes and I arch into the touch. I find the center of my desire, the need just below the surface.

My release hovers near the edge waiting for the right instant to quiver and crash throughout my body. I silence the first pleasured cry but when my dorm room door opens and my roommate walks in, the gasp of horror ripped from my throat is more the sound of a strangled pelican.

The candles dance in the sudden rush of air. I grab for the covers but can't hide.

I've been caught.

Heat, both from my humiliation and from the need still coursing through my body, explode over my face.

"Oh, god."

My voice shakes. It honest to god shakes.

Lily's delicious smile plays on her lips like a smoky refrain of smooth jazz. Her boyfriend, Jon, peers over her shoulder, a similar smile tugging up the corner of his mouth. The duet winds around my insides, and pulses staccato beats of pleasure between my legs.

I couldn't be more mortified if they'd discovered me stealing money from the Sunday collection plate or eating their leftover lo Mein.

"I'm so sorry." The apology quivers on my lips. I clutch the sheet to my neck but want to dive underneath.

I don't, strangely enough. Curiosity drives me to see their reactions.

"I didn't think you'd be back tonight."

Lily favors me with an uninhibited appraisal though beneath the cover I don't think she can see all that much. "Don't apologize on my account."

The molten heat in the depths of her dark, reveal-nothing eyes sears my flesh but her smile is not one of evil mischief.

It's one of interest.

What. The. Fuck? She's messing with me, obviously. *Switzerland*, I remind myself.

Behind her, Jon closes the door and I hear the lock click into place. I should have been so smart.

Lily shrugs out of the leather coat poured over her lithe frame, revealing a white tank top beneath. She's not wearing a bra, her breasts firm and perfectly rounded and I can see the circles of her areolas beneath the thin cotton. Her nipples are a dark beacon of temptation.

"Or on my account," Jon chimes in. He presses close

behind her, hands on her slender waist, pulling her against him. I can only guess why and my still humming sexual need gives a little zing at the thought.

She tugs at the sheet I clutch to my near naked body. I pull back, grasping the shield tighter to my breasts.

She *tsks* reproachfully. "Don't get shy, now."

Heat explodes throughout my entire body, blossoming from a central core located between my legs. The mushroom cloud chases all thoughts out of my head. I dry swallow the heartbeat throbbing in my throat.

"Please continue, Bree."

Bree. It's a name only she uses. She says my given name, Gabrielle, is too stuffy and that I need a name that drifts free like a breeze. But that's not me.

Or is it?

She props one knee on the end of my bed, studying me behind hooded eyes, a cougar stalking her prey. Muscles bunch and flex against the painted-on-denim of her jeans, coiled restraint waiting to be released.

Her voice rolls my abbreviated name from her throat like the purr of the contented feline she embodies, and an image of her cat-like tongue on my tingling flesh surges in my brain.

Words fail me. I do manage a brief shake of my head. No way was I putting on a show. I didn't like being the center of attention when I was a kid forced into piano recitals and dance recitals or show-off-the-adopted-niece family gatherings. I certainly wasn't performing for an audience now. Almost naked, no less.

"No?" She pouts her lip and *tsks* at me again.

Damn I love that sound. And that look, made all the sultrier when issued beneath the probing stare. Long lashes fan over wide eyes tilted slightly up at the corners, giving her a look of perpetual curiosity.

She invades my physical space more intimately than anyone I'd ever known.

"Maybe I can watch another time then."

She finger-walks her right hand toward the foot peeking out from beneath my boring blue comforter. Lily makes a move to touch the arch, but I withdraw it from her reach.

She gifts me with that smile again. "Perhaps you'll even let me help."

What thoughts manage to flow into my paralyzed brain screech to a grinding halt. Too bad my body still works overtime. *Help? She wants to help* me? The walls of my sex clutch and release, waiting for more.

Wanting more.

"I...I don't understand."

Lily pulls the other knee up on the edge of the bed, sitting back on her heels, and tugs at the sheet again. The long fingers of her hands twine around the cotton, nails painted a brilliant metallic purple that winks and sparkles in the dim light.

This time I let the hand holding the cover fall below my breasts.

Over her shoulder, I see Jon's eyes narrow and his lips part slightly. He bites the lower lip and the breath rasps in, then out.

"I think you do, sweet Bree."

My nipples spring to life. Breathing is difficult. I sit face to face with not just *one* of my fantasies.

But *the* fantasy.

Not one I would ever admit to, not even in my diary. But

the thought of being adventurous, just once, battles inhibitions borne from the void of my non-existent sex life.

Can I let this happen?

She shimmies her hips and leans forward and again I think of a cat waiting to pounce. She props one hand at my waist, her face now just inches from mine. Our breaths mix, a heady cocktail of spearmint and lust.

Whether she senses my silent approval or not, she lifts her hand to the edge of the sheet near my breasts and works it from my grasp, sliding it down my body to reveal my bare legs.

One finger trails beneath the cover, scorching a path down my torso and against the thigh. My flesh dimples at her touch and a thousand points of desire rise in eager anticipation. A ribbon of fire originates from her fingertip and blazes right to the ache between my thighs.

Lily slides her hands down the inside curve of my upper leg, pressing only slightly until my thighs fall open. "Lie back."

The command touches something inside of me, something unknown. Something I want but cannot name.

The whiskey hoarseness to her voice soothes me. I do as she asks without question. I want her against me. I want to feel her breath scorch the tender, almost virginal flesh between my thighs. I'd been with one man – and I use the term generously - in my twenty-four years.

He'd not made an impression.

As if pulled by my thoughts Jon walks silently to the other side of the room, giving me an unfettered look at an ass that could make even the most boring tighty whities look hot.

He collapses on Lily's bed, crossing his long legs at the ankles and resting his weight back on the elbows. The light of the candles reflects in his eyes, pinpricks of gold amidst a mossy backdrop.

He looks solidly built but not overly muscular, his body that of a runner or a swimmer – long, sleek. Wide shoulders fill out the black t-shirt and the tightly tucked cotton reveals a flat, hard stomach.

The front of his button-fly jeans tent alluringly, the denim straining to hold back whatever lies beneath. Our eyes meet and his hand cups the swell. A small, knowing nod.

Warmth cascades over my flesh at the promise in his eyes and that small nod.

Lily skims her knuckles over my breasts, tracing circles around the dark centers, and brings my attention back to her. "I hear you at night."

Again the heat in my face and body flush as my eyes lock with hers. The thought of Lily lying only a few feet away, listening as I masturbate floods my face with shame... and desire.

"You do?" Something brave rouses in that moment. "What do you hear?"

My question elicits a smile. "I hear you call my name." She looks over her shoulder and Jon's face melts into a puddle of adoration. "And Jon's."

Her attention returns to me as she rises from the bed, her body long and lean, invitation wrapped in gold skin and delivered on a sultry smile. She kicks out of her shoes and shimmies out of the skinny jeans hugging every delectable curve.

Sheer ivory undies accentuate slender hips and reveal a neatly trimmed pubis. Compared to her, I look like a chia pet.

If I'd known all my fantasies would come true tonight,

I'd have made an extra stop at the mall. At least I shaved my legs this morning.

Ever in tune to my wayward thoughts, she tips my chin back with a single touch until my eyes return to hers. "Jon fucks me harder when I tell him about you."

ANTICIPATION
CHAPTER THREE

Lily melts back onto the bed, tugging the edge of her white cotton tank down a bit. It plays peek-a-boo with the pierced belly button, a double-ended diamond stud flush against the soft buttery skin.

It's sexier somehow that she's not completely naked. She's a present waiting to be unwrapped. And it's Christmas morning.

She cocks her hip to the side and splays her fingers over the flat plane of her belly, pushing downward until her hands dive between her thighs. "I can't even be jealous because I feel the same."

My fingers curl into the sheet pooled around me, wanting to pull the covers up over my face and hide. Masturbating while she slept just a few feet away had been my dirty little secret, or so I thought. Her confession is a shock and a turn on. "I didn't know you could hear me."

She slides back onto the bed, tucking the long legs beneath her ass. High, muscled calves flex as she adjusts her position. I wondered what they would feel like wrapped around my waist.

"You're so quiet. I'm sure you thought you were safe in the darkness," she continues, scooting up the bed then moving between my outstretched legs. "I thought maybe you were a virgin, but then," Lily leans forward, bracing first one hand then the other on each side of my body. She lets the tip of her cotton covered breasts touch mine. A sizzle arcs between our bodies like two ends of a live wire. "I decided that you'd just never been properly fucked."

Her face hovers above mine; I could have closed the distance in a heartbeat. Each rasp of her breath mingles with my own ragged pants.

"So, tell me, Bree." She glances down the line of our bodies, her eyes touching intimately in places, hovering in promise at others. "Have you ever been properly fucked?"

I want to scream out, *Yes*. But my body betrays my pride. My single foray into the world of carnal pleasure had been a disaster. I wasn't even sure he'd broken my cherry, if such a thing existed.

"N-no," I manage to stammer. The confession embarrasses me as much as getting caught with my hand between my thighs.

"Say it." Her hand snakes out and she grasps my chin, holding my attention in an unyielding but gentle grip.

The command leaves me stunned. I swallow the lump in my throat, feeling my face burn before the words cross my tongue. "I've never been properly fucked."

Her tongue darts out and tastes the cupid's bow of my upper lip as she releases me. "Would you like to be?"

"Yes." The word rushes out before I can think. She quirks that smile at me again, the one that curls the edge of her lip, the one with promise.

She kisses me, softly at first, a simple tasting as if trying a new dish to decide if you like it. Then the kiss deepens and her tongue slithers along the edge of my teeth, teasing and chasing my hesitant tongue. A moan trembles in my throat; husky, wanton.

"Trust yourself, Bree," Lily murmurs between kisses, her lips everywhere at once, stirring senses I didn't know existed inside of me.

But I didn't trust myself, reliving in seconds the long succession of losers I'd trusted with my heart, only to have it trampled, ignored, and later forgotten. That was why I'd waited for the "right" man.

Only he'd been the biggest loser of them all. Fuck, tuck, and duck summed up our relationship. I was still in bed, my body aching with unfulfilled desire, when he closed the door on the way out of the motel room I'd put on my maxed out credit card.

I swore off men after that. Maybe I was a lesbian, I'd decided but hadn't been brave enough to explore that side of my sexuality. Until now. Jon, sitting just a few feet away, his cock bulging beneath the tight denim, put a new twist even on that.

"I'm not sure I know how to trust myself."

Lily presses her lips against my cheek, then against my ear. "I can help with that, too."

When I dare, I move my mouth to hers and let my tongue roam between her lips. She captures the tip between her teeth. While we hover there, precariously joined, she slips her hand beneath the whisper of lace covering my pussy, probing the outer layers until I relax and let her touch slide between the folds of my labia. She releases my mouth as my breath catches and I inhale sharply as her middle finger slips easily into my body.

"She's so tight, Jon," Lily announces, all the while holding my gaze with her own. The walls of my vagina suck at the welcome intrusion. "I can't wait for you to feel this."

"Neither can I," Jon answers, and I meet his eyes over Lily's shoulder. He rests on one elbow, the other hand rubbing over the bulge in his jeans.

Lily finds the swollen nub of my clit with the pad of her thumb and my attention snaps back to her and the connection between our bodies. She massages the pleasure point in agonizingly slow circles.

I arch into her touch, biting my lip to silence the cries of sinful lust. Just as the first ripple of release begins a crescendo through my body, Lily withdraws her finger from my slick folds, cupping the juncture at my thighs with her hand.

"Not yet," she whispers.

"Why not?" I cry out, then purse my lips to silence. "Sorry."

She traces the bow of my lip with the finger she'd removed from my body, the musk of my own desire still damp on her skin. "Stop apologizing." She tugs on my lower lip until I open my mouth and slips her finger inside. "Taste."

I flick my tongue tentatively against the tip and taste the salty tang of my own desire. Then I wrap my lips around her finger and suck it into my mouth completely.

"See how sweet that is?" She kisses me around her finger, tasting me two ways. "I don't want to rush anything tonight. I want to savor it all."

She removes her finger from my mouth, and I sit there while she coaxes the straps of the teddy from my shoulders. "Let's get rid of this first."

I sit up, breathless in anticipation, my heart hammering in my chest, the pulsing also lower in my body. My weight rests on my hands. Jon watches from the dark. I can barely make out his face through the shadows of dancing candle-light, but a glimmer catches on his watch and I see his hand move in slow, measured strokes beneath the open 'V' of his jeans. What little breath I have left snags in my lungs.

"If I'm a distraction, I can wait outside." He offers but doesn't move his hand.

And again, what little breath filling my lungs catches and fuels the explosion of heat coursing through my limbs. I didn't want him to leave but can only shake my head.

"Good. Because I want to see you come." He pauses dramatically, as if to wait for the right moment. Then adds, "Often."

I might have orgasmed right then and there, but Lily pulls the teddy down my body and I focus on telling my muscles what to do. I lift my hips from the bed with her still situated between my thighs. The sizzle of contact – my wetness to her hard nipples – skims along my nerves, a tidal wave of moisture over electric wires.

She glances back to Jon and tosses the teddy in his direction. He plucks it from the corner of the bed, bundles the non-existent fabric in his free hand and holds it to his face, inhaling deeply then nuzzling the fabric like a contented cat. Jon burrows his nose deeper but keeps his eyes on us over the red silk.

"Save a little for me," he laughs and I'm not sure which of us he's speaking to. His eyes dance between us. "I want my share."

Lily wiggles her ass in the air and her full breasts sway with the playful motion. "There's plenty for you anytime you're ready."

Jon's head lolls back slightly. "I'm going to get some of that, too."

I'm both intrigued and frightened by the events unfolding in my dorm room. It's a dream, I try and convince myself. I've fallen asleep in the quiet of the building and now I'm having an incredibly hot sex dream. It's the only logical explanation because Lily poised between my thighs defies logic.

I'm wet and throbbing in places that have never been as alive as they are right at this moment. If it's a dream, I don't want to wake up. Ever.

Lily returns her attention to me and I forget about Jon... for the moment.

Naked now, completely vulnerable, I meet Lily's intensely penetrating gaze. A dark flush stains her cheeks, large pupils dilated to black diamonds ringed in melted caramel. She kisses me and there's no urge to pull away. I kiss her back, playing my tongue against the probing presence of hers.

Feeling a little braver, I ease my hand beneath the hem of her tank top. Her ribs rise and fall with each breath I feel against my face. My fingertips brush against the under-curve of her breast and I slide my hand further until the swell of her bare breast fills my palm.

Goosebumps jump to life beneath my fingers. Her nipples harden, the skin around them tight and puckered. I capture one of the swollen tips between my thumb and forefinger and tweak it gently. She gasps slightly and I smile. There is an immense power in bringing her pleasure.

Her mouth traces a line along my jaw, down the slope of my neck to the hollow at my throat. Warmth follows her touch and continues a path to parts of my body still humming from my own masturbation moments ago, though it feels a lifetime now. She pushes me down, bracing her weight on each side of my body as she lowers her head toward me. As her lips trail over the arch of my breast I am caught by a wave of sudden uncertainty.

My shoulders tighten but not with pleasure or desire. Lily looks up, concern crinkling at the corners of her sultry mouth.

The air is heavy; the echo of my pounding heart carried on the tension. Newspaper headlines flash behind my eyes.

Coed Expelled for Dorm Sex Triangle

Coed Found Dead; Roommate, Boyfriend suspected

I look over to Jon and he's picked up on my hesitation. He leans into the light. He doesn't strike me as the murderous type, really. A body to die for, maybe.

Jon gives me a little wink, but his face is all serious. "All you have to do is say stop, Bree. We won't go any further than you want."

I look back to Lily and read the same assurance in her face.

"Seriously. Just say stop. No hard feelings, ok? We want you," and she pauses, closes her eyes, then continues on a deep exhale of breath, "*Really* want you, but I know it can be overwhelming. We can try again another night or not at all. It's all up to you."

They've given me no reason to doubt them. I mean, I met her parents when she moved into the dorm. Jon's sister visits her here on a regular basis. And besides, my overly cautious little voice whispers, the walls are so thin I'm going to have to worry more about *not* being heard than someone ignoring my struggles if I'm being murdered. The dorm is quiet but not empty.

My next breath is deep, cleansing, and the hesitation dissipates from my body with the release of air. The stiffness along my spine eases and I relax back against the bed. Lily brushes her cheek against mine in a gesture more intimate than I had ever experienced. So much in that simple touch.

"We won't harm you. I promise." Then, seconds later, "Possibly just a little sweet pain."

Her breath rushes against my ear and I'm certain I hear her heart beating in rhythm to mine. Those words, that promise, it's everything I want and need and nothing I expect. Tonight, though, I'm taking the chance.

I always play it safe, do the practical thing. Tonight, I'll take a risk.

Or two, I amend and look at Jon. Mornings are for regrets. I'll deal with them when I must. And frankly, I expect I'll have to at some point. It's not like this will be a lifetime choice.

DARE
CHAPTER FOUR

M aking eye contact, I give her a nod.
"Yes?"

Her own body relaxes as she trails hot kisses down the arc of my neck, across the ridge of my shoulders.

"You don't sound certain." Her tongue flicks deliciously quick at the spot beneath my jaw where my pulse quivers. My heart jumps with each connection, every flash of heat pulsing like electricity to the ends of my fingers and toes.

I close my eyes and let my body rise to meet her sweet mouth. Soon she is back to the swell of my breast and this time, instead of hesitation, I am impatient to feel her mouth upon my skin.

"Yes." The voice is mine, certain, strong, but it comes from someplace inside me I don't recognize.

I tangle my hands in her hair and pull her closer. She circles one areola with her tongue, tracing the outline.

"Definitely yes."

Lily gently takes the nipple between her teeth, pulling it upward then releasing it to continue her journey down my torso. My stomach tightens as she circles my belly button.

My breathing stops as she adjusts her body down the bed, watching me watch her.

"Do you want me to kiss you here?" she asks, teasing, nestling her chin in the little hollow where my tummy dips down to my pubis.

I nod, unable to find any air to make my vocal cords work.

Next she nuzzles the inside of my thigh with her mouth. "You can do better than that, Bree."

Lily moves a little closer to the target but doesn't go in for the kill. Two fingers dance across the juncture where my thighs meet my pussy, as if looking for a partner for some forbidden samba.

"Do you want me to kiss you—" Her chin presses over my clit, a delicious pressure point. "Here?"

"Yes," the word rushes out. Quickly followed by, "Yes. Please."

Then my world explodes as her fingers part the sensitive flesh, her head dips and she laps it for the first time with her tongue.

A tortured gasp erupts from my throat as she teases the soft folds with agonizing slowness.

"Oh, god."

Jon's deep laugh ripples across the room. "I don't think she likes that, Lily."

Lily's head tilts back just enough for our eyes to meet over the curve of my body. "Her pussy says differently."

"The pussy is always right."

I can't find my breath but my heart settles between my legs as Lily dips her head back and the heat of her breath and tongue find my body again. The pulsating throb is intense, vibrating through my body and exploding behind my closed eyes. She lavishes long, slow kisses on the flesh, taking my clit in her mouth, sucking, tugging, teasing.

The enormity of what Lily is doing creeps along the outer edges of my thoughts, but I can summon neither shame nor regret. For the first time, I know what people mean when they say, *It just feels right*.

I am meant for this, my body curved just right to accept the softness of another woman against my own. But another longing hovers just outside the lust induced fog of my brain. A longing to feel the steady thrusts of a man pushing deep into my body, filling all the empty places within. I can't rectify the opposing desires and don't work too hard at trying. Lily's mouth is heaven.

"I wish you could see her face, Lil," Jon announces, rising off the bed to move closer to us. "If ecstasy has an expression, she's wearing it."

I am barely coherent, unable to focus long on any thought for the swirl of desire coursing across my flesh. My head falls back, my eyes close. Lily doesn't linger overlong on any one spot, igniting dozens of firestorms along the juncture of my thighs. I reach down with my right hand and tangle my fingers in Lily's silky hair, wanting to feel more of her than the tip of her tongue, the flick of a finger, wanting her to know the pleasure she brings. She dips her tongue in my crease and I am lost again.

The creak of a bed breaks my concentration momentarily and I open my eyes. Jon is kneeling on the bed, one hand resting on Lily's ass, his gaze riveted to her movements. His cock juts out from the vee of his opened jeans, and I am awestruck at the size – the thick, dark head a glorious crown over the smooth length.

My body gives a delightful shudder at the thought of him pointing that in my direction. He's pulled the front of the t-shirt high enough to see the matting of darker hair leading my eyes downward. He's commando and that thought makes me lick my lips.

Our time will come, he seemed to say earlier. Is it wishful thinking on my part? While my one sexual encounter had been disappointing, I never attributed it to anything but my own inhibitions that left me incapable of relaxation during the act. Maybe size is everything. And if not size, then experience must certainly play a part.

I think Jon will settle both questions.

He rings the shaft with a fist, palming the length and circling the head with his thumb. A deep purple vein runs the length, twisting like a snake from the hairy root to the dark tip. Jon circles the head slowly in his fist, closing his eyes to some inner thought. Is he thinking of Lily? Me? I try not to dwell on that hopeful thought.

Jon pulls the back of the t-shirt from the waistband of his jeans, lifts it over his head and drops it to the floor. I see the washboard abs I suspected hiding beneath his clothes, the ridged line of muscles a sharp contrast on his skin. He pushes the jeans down and leaves the puddle of denim on the floor.

He holds a condom in his left hand and tears open the cellophane wrapper and rolls the thin sheath on his erection. He reaches down again and tugs at the sac hanging heavily between his muscular thighs, a sigh rushing from his body. He tugs at it again, this time more in control.

I follow him with my eyes as he moves behind Lily. She is crouched between my outspread thighs, her head low, her ass high. Ten thousand nerve endings are jumping at the magic Lily is performing on my clit but they hitch up another notch as I realize what Jon is about to do.

She looks up, her eyes huge and dark, a little glazed.

"Damn Jon, I don't know what you're doing but she's creaming all over me at the thought of it. Keep it up, will you?"

He laughs, a deep, relaxed sound that fills my tiny room. "My pleasure," then he bends over her back and reaches around with one hand to cup her breasts in his palm. I can feel his knuckles brush my thighs as he grasps her nipples. My own harden and I want to feel his hands and lips on my body.

Jon traces the outline of her panties with his finger then pulls the white cotton down. He urges her legs apart and she complies. I thought myself on the edge of oblivion already but seeing Jon poised to take Lily from behind kicks up the level of my own adrenaline.

I know when he pushes into her because of Lily's quick intake of breath against my own body. I gasp with surprise as Jon begins to thrust into Lily. The pulse of their joining transfers through the ministration of Lily's mouth on my flesh.

She returns her attention to my clit and the direct stimulation on the engorged nub brings me to the brink. I teeter on the edge only briefly. With only a few swirls of her tongue I shudder my release not just once or twice, but four deep spasms roll over and through my body. I drown beneath the waves of pleasure, slowly coming back to the surface of reality.

"Fuck," I whisper reverentially. It is the only word appropriate to the lightning emotions striking every nerve ending I possess.

Smaller ripples skim along my raw nerves, skittering like aftershocks across my skin.

As I drift back, I watch Lily and Jon, lost in their own world for the moment. Their bodies move in sync with each other. Jon kisses the curve of her shoulder, one hand curling beneath Lily's ass.

Whatever he's doing brings a gasp from her. She arches her ass higher and murmurs words in a language I don't recognize. He answers against her ear.

I don't know the language, but I know the words. Words of love and passion and connection. Their heads rest side by side as their bodies come together.

I am not jealous because of their rapt attention with each other, strangely enough. Nor do I feel an intruder. I am part of their world even if only for this brief time and that comfort is foreign to me as what I am doing naked in bed with these two people.

I slide up the bed a bit and twist around, then angle myself against the wall so I can see beneath Lily's torso. Her full breasts sway with the motion of Jon's thrusts. He's tweaking her nipples between his forefinger and thumb, a gesture I had also used. I push myself further down until I can see Jon's shaft sliding in and out of Lily's slit. That rush of uncertainty threatens again but I stamp it back.

I touch Lily tentatively and hear a quick "yes" from her, so I circle my thumb and index finger around Jon's thrusting shaft. They both gasp at the contact and since their movements do not lessen, I continue my exploration. Lily is bared for my view, her clit swollen, body slick. Gently I caress her, surprised when her clit throbs against my novice fingers.

I hear Lily rasp another quick "Yes" as I massage the quivering flesh. She is wet and my fingers slide over her easily. I move my other hand around the back of her thighs to cup the weighty sac of Jon's testicles. They draw up at first contact and I wonder if I've done something wrong, but I feel a hand between my own legs and look down to see Jon's hand cupping the juncture at my thighs. He parts the flesh and my own passions reignite as he slips his middle finger into my still sensitive sheath and finds my clit with his thumb.

I didn't think it was possible, but I knew I would come again. I hoped it would be in union with Lily and Jon.

Lily's gasps come quicker and quicker, her fingers curling into the sheet as if they are the only thing keeping her on the bed. "Harder, Jon." A sharp intake of breath. "Harder."

Jon tangles his free hand in her hair and pulls back, her neck arcing long and slender. His thrusts quicken as he chases after the same pleasure hovering just out of reach, fingering my flesh with the agility of a concert pianist. I lift my hips in sync to his movements, churning against the rising heat in my belly.

Lily and I cry out together with the first burst of pleasure, Jon's following only a split second later. But he keeps pounding into Lily, pleasured agony tightening the lines around his mouth and eyes. Minutes later, another orgasm tightens my body and elicits a tortured, deep throated moan I don't recognize as being my own. Jon and Lily strangle out a cry in unison in harmony with my own.

His rhythm begins to slow, and he releases Lily's hair, then cradles her head in his palm. Lily shudders again and her body goes limp. I press a brief kiss to her hip then slide back around to the top of the bed so she can collapse.

She falls facing me, her flushed face and rock-hard nipples a tribute to the pleasure she found. Jon falls in behind me and I lay sandwiched between them, the warmth sliding over me like a comforter. Jon lays one hand on my shoulder, his fingers brushing both Lily's breast and mine. He drapes the other arm over my waist and snuggles me closer. Again, the silent promise of things yet to come.

When the doubts push forward, I kick them from my mind. There would be time for that later. I fall asleep, sated, warm and content.

HESITATION
CHAPTER FIVE

I wake sometime later, one hour, three hours, more; I don't know. Outside my third story window, the threat of morning isn't even a hint in the sky visible behind the light sheers hanging from the valence. I turn in the warm cocoon of Jon and Lily's bodies to face Jon. I peer straight into the lush green of emeralds and thick pine forests.

It takes a second for the image to register – for my vision to pull back and take in the entire picture. The sharp slash of his brows a darker shade of brown than his hair. The angles of his cheeks and jawline. The fuzz of a beard just starting to show. A deep cleft splits his chin. The slightly crooked way his bottom lip sets off from his upper lip. I'm definitely not used to waking up next to someone. And not someone so damned intriguing.

"Hi," he whispers, his voice more of a caress than a sound.

"Hi." I try to sound seductive and wanton, but I secretly hope my breath doesn't reek.

"I'm going to take a shower. Want to join me?"

I open my mouth to say yes, then pause. He is Lily's

boyfriend/significant other. I'm...what? I haven't a clue. Jon's mind reading skills are top notch luckily.

"She won't mind. Lil sleeps like the dead for hours and I'm not ready to call it a night."

"He's probably already hard," Lily murmurs in a sleep-heavy voice, snuggling deeper into the covers.

True enough, the curve of Jon's hardening cock brushes against my stomach. My body responds first, filling with the liquid heat of my own desire. I nod, a warm blush creeping up my neck.

Jon grins at my shyness then takes my hand and yanks me from the bed with an exaggerated grunt. Lily rolls into the warm void left by us, pulling the covers beneath her breasts. Jon tosses something into the shower tub hanging on the back of the door then grabs it and the towels without losing stride. He unlocks the door and, without even a hint of reluctance, walks into the hallway buck naked, me in tow.

My heart starts to beat, and I remember to breathe about the time I realize the hall is deserted. The wall clock tells me it's a little after four.

My world has completely changed in less than six hours.

I remain silent in my shock. Luckily, it's only a short walk to the showers, but a longer walk would be just fine because Jon's ass is quite nice from this point of view.

Taut cheeks, the slight hollow of muscle on the sides dimpling with each step. His waist tapers to sturdy yet slender legs and calves. I want to be entwined with those limbs and held prisoner beneath their weight and strength while Jon has his way with me, any way he wants.

Geez, I mentally slap myself. One night of killer sex and I'm fantasizing about actually having a sex life.

"Like the view?" He says over his shoulder, not even looking back to confirm his suspicions that I'm oogling his backside.

That blush I'd felt earlier mushrooms to nuclear. "Well, yeah," I answer, surprised by the words. Who am I? He turns but doesn't stop walking, a look of shock at my admission. I shrug. "You want me to lie?"

His head dips with the quiet laugh. "Never," then he squeezes my hand and pushes open the door to the bathroom, going straight to the shower furthermost from the door. The bathrooms are gender neutral, all the showers and toilets in self-contained units that lock.

The interior of the stall is dark and, being on the end, a little roomier than the other three.

"Did you know this stall is bigger from experience or just an educated guess?" I slid the shower curtain closed, then turn to see him stash the shower bucket inside and hang the towels.

"What do you think?" He towers over me, not imposing his height but using it to wrap his nearness around me. A ghost of a smile tugs at the corner of his mouth, deepening the cleft in his chin.

Damn that chin is sexy. He lowers his head and the scent of some cologne or soap lingers around him, but it's Lil's scent I want to lick directly from his skin.

"Definitely experience." I look up into his face, my words raspy and ragged.

"Smart girl."

And he kisses me.

Our lips light upon one another but don't move at first, a sweet mingling of breath. The heat from his body swirls around me and when he breaks the kiss, I'm left cold, empty.

He's not yours, I remind myself. But I really don't want to linger on the thought. He's mine for now.

Jon twists on the water and adjusts the temperature then leads me beneath the pulsing spray. He pulls me close and nuzzles my neck, nibbling at my earlobe and the hollow just beneath. My hands are trapped between us, holding him back while at the same time keeping me internally balanced.

Can't fall for Lily's boyfriend, becomes my mantra.

The warm water mists off his shoulders so I shut my eyes, leaning into his touch.

"You're so sweet," he murmurs close into my ear. His breath skims along my face. "I've dreamed about you, taking you like this, holding you close." His hands slide down my neck to cup my face and lift it to his. This time his kiss is demanding, forceful, consuming. I let him have me.

I open my mouth to his probing tongue and let my hands slide down his torso, curving around his back to clutch the hard swell of his buttocks. I urge him a little closer. He readily acquiesces.

His cock is hard, trapped between our bodies. Jon reaches down and positions his shaft between my thighs. The length rubs the crease of my body, the light pressure tantalizing, as insistent as his kiss.

Jon steps back and pulls me directly beneath the spray of water. Rivulets cascade from my neck and shoulders, passing over and between my breasts. The warmth lulls my body and mind and I let more tension slip away with the running water.

"Can I bathe you?"

"Only if I can return the favor." The brazen retort surprises me again. I do not want to be a bystander any longer.

"There will be time for that later. For now, I want to concentrate on you."

I'd never been the center of anyone's attention, and I immediately go to ask *why* but I quiet the usual nagging voice of doubt. No one has ever really done anything nice for me without expecting more in return. My uncle took me in after my parents' deaths because he thought he'd get his hands on his brother's money. When he didn't, I paid the price.

But Jon and I have no such history. His face is the epitome of sincerity and I admit, his words touch a part of me deeper than my sex. The cynic in me wonders what Jon and Lily will want and what it will cost me when they leave.

Jon grasps my chin in his palm and brings my gaze up to meet his.

"I can hear your mind turning and spinning, Gabrielle. Don't try to figure it all out tonight. There'll be time." He kisses the tip of my nose, the hollow beneath my jaw, then rests his cheek against mine and just holds me while I wrestle with the inner demons.

I drag in a breath, focus on the line of connection between our bodies then draw back from Jon and kiss him. He smiles as our lips touch and I can't help but smile back.

"All better?" he asks, as if he knows the inner argument I wage.

"Better." It's not perfect but then nothing ever is. You can only enjoy the moment and I'm determined to do just that.

He retrieves the liquid soap and lathers the body puff. Jon starts at the base of my throat, making slow circles across the ridge of my shoulders then moving down to each breast.

My nipples harden and despite the warmth of the

water, I shudder as his hand trails lower to my abdomen. Jon pays careful attention to my thighs and calves, even my feet receive special attention. Everything except the part of me I most want him to touch.

As he turns me in the circle of his arms, I let disappointment pout on my lips to his amusement, but it quickly fades as he leans against me, the hardness of his cock settling against my stomach. He raises my hands over my head and pins my wrists to the wall.

The restraint panics me instantly – my heart races and a breath catches like a sticky lump in my throat - and I try and pull my hands away. It must catch him off guard because he doesn't release me right away and that moment of hesitation makes me curl in on myself once I'm free.

I'd fought carefully in my life to be the one in control, so I resist. It is the only thing that comes natural to me.

I wrap my arms around my waist and press myself against the cool tile.

"It's ok," he assures me over and over again stepping back, giving me space even in the small confines of the shower stall. When I turn to meet his eyes again, he smiles. "Can I come closer?"

I nod, still uncertain, trembling beneath his touch and I curse the anxiety taking over once again. Jon moves forward slightly and the heat of his body pulses around me. He murmurs words of comfort and apology and I feel like shit for ruining the moment.

"I'm going to touch your forehead," he whispers, and brushes a damp strand of hair back. "And your ear." He tucks the hair behind the shell of my ear. "Your neck." He's closer now. "And I can wrap you in a towel and carry you back to bed never regretting for one instant we did nothing more than this." A feathery kiss.

I suck in a deep breath and mentally force the tension from my limbs. I turn my face to him, the words to explain my fears dancing on my tongue.

He smiles, sincerity wafting off him. "It's all right, sweetness."

Hot water haloes off his shoulders and mists around his face. Mossy green eyes darken like turbulent waters, the pupil lost in the ebon of his soulful expression. I'd known this man only in brief interludes but something inside of me tells me I can trust him. But I no longer trust that little voice. It had led me wrong before.

"We can go back to the room, curl up with Lily." He raises a hand to brush a wet piece of hair from my face but lowers it. His movements are languid, the tone of his voice quiet, calm.

I shake my head. "Can we try again?"

He puffs his chest and waggles his eyebrows in an exaggerated and completely fake leer. I almost laugh at the gesture but still feel like shit for killing the moment.

"Anytime you want, Bree." Then he widens his stance and plants his fists at his hips, very much the Superman pose. "I'm at your service, ma'am."

He gives me a little wink and this time the laughter that bubbles up is genuine, relaxed. Then I'm sure about what I say next.

"Now?"

VENTURE
CHAPTER SIX

H e cocks his head to the side a bit, body posture relaxing, questioning me with raised brows.

"I'm sure."

He studies my face, then nods, a half-smile lifting the corner of that sexy mouth. This time when he reaches up to brush the hair from my face, he follows through but threads his hand into my hair and cups the back of my neck. We make some serious eye contact and that invisible touch goes all the way to my toes.

"If at any time, and I do mean *any* time," he stresses, "you feel uncomfortable or don't like where we're going, say yellow. That'll be a clue we need to slow down, ask questions, reposition, change tactics. If you say red, I'll stop immediately. No questions asked. No guilt on your part. No anger or resentment on mine. None." He massages the muscles at the nape of my neck. "Okay?"

I can do this; I urge myself mentally.

I nod once, answering both my question and Jon's. "Okay."

"Raise your arms."

I did as Jon asked with only a slight hesitation.

Jon waits a breath then moves his hands up the inside of my outstretched arms until our palms are mated but he doesn't link our fingers.

He guides me into position facing the shower wall. My hands are braced above my head shoulder width apart, fingers splayed against the cool tile, legs slightly back. He releases my hands and trails a path against my skin down my arms, across my shoulders. His hands circle my waist then continue around to my stomach. A quick nuzzle of my earlobe and he moves back.

I hear things move around in the shower bucket then he begins again with the bath at the nape of my neck, moving across each shoulder blade and down the ridge of my spine. As he moves across the arc of my ass his fingers slide around the wall of my sex. The muscles contract and he sucks in a deep breath.

"God, you are beautiful." He makes another slow circuit around the heated edge of my pussy. "I couldn't wait to get inside you and my little finger-fuck earlier only made me want you more. Can I have you, Gabrielle?"

Breathless, I simply nod. He releases me and I hear the rattle of items in the shower buck, the rip of cellophane.

He plants his palms on each side of my own and nudges his knee between my thighs until my legs part more. His hands trail down my arms, pausing to cup my breasts and tweak the nipples with his thumb and forefinger. Much like he had with Lily, Jon cups my sex with one hand and uses the other to guide his cock to the entrance to my body.

The tip of his cock brushes the edge of my sex, dipping shallow into the wetness of my body a few times. I take a preliminary deep breath to calm my nerves.

"All good?" He asks, not stopping what he is doing but not going any further.

I think of his words earlier. Yellow for caution. Red for stop. I take it to the next natural step. "Green."

And with that he pushes himself just inside my aching body as gently as possible, using his hold on my sex as an anchor and as a distraction.

I gasp at the intrusion. I'm no virgin but my body rebels at the pressure and size of him. The pressure is just this side of pain, a burn that tingles and swirls and coils like a slow rising heat.

He pauses and withdraws slightly, the void almost as painful as the initial penetration. I whimper my distress.

"You like that, don't you?"

"Yes," I cry out through the fog of need as he enters me again, slightly more than before. The slow heat builds and wraps itself tighter around my insides.

He uses the hand cupping my sex to find my clit and put pressure just above it, the hollow more sensitive than I could ever have guessed. I gasp, a strangled sound, and start to move against his fingers but he stops me with the weight of his body.

"One day I'll make you beg for more."

He circles the clit with his finger once, twice. Agonizingly, blissfully slow circles.

"And I'll be a bastard and say no."

My brain tries to focus on his words, on the movement of his lips against my ear but my entire thought process is centered on where our bodies are joined.

More pressure, brief, titillating as he rocks forward, driving his cock deeper into my body. The wave of orgasm pushes forward, a rolling avalanche gaining momentum.

"In fact, I won't let you come at all. Maybe for days. I'll just do this."

He pumps into me again, deeper still.

"Tonight, I want you to ask me for more, knowing you'll get what you ask for."

I cry out before my brain overthinks it. "Please, Jon,"

"Please what, Bree?"

Another delicious circle. Another strong push with his hips. But just one.

"Please do that again." And he did. Just one painfully, deliciously slow circle around my clit. One strong pump with the length of his cock. The bastard. The sharp edge of pleasure draws a strangled cry from a deep part of my chest. I turn my head and see his face so close to mine, the humor a glint in his eyes. I shoot him an evil look.

"What?"

Innocence does not work on this man. He is sin on a silver platter.

"You know what." I push back against his hips, wanting all of him inside of me.

"I gave you exactly what you asked for." Jon increases the pressure on my clit, and I suck in a breath. "If you want more, ask for it."

Such a simple request but the words tangle in my brain. Asking for things can be dangerous, costly. Stupid lessons I knew didn't apply here – he'd even told me I'd get what I asked for - but lessons I'd learned too well. I lean back, resting my temple against his chin.

He presses his lips against the side of my cheek and whispers, "It's ok," then thrusts his hips slowly forward, pushing past the innocence left by one inept lover. "You'll get there."

I gasp and press my hand over Jon's still holding my sex. Our fingers find my clit but he controls the motion, unwilling to let me rush towards the growing explosion.

He pulls out again, slowly, expertly letting the head of his erection caress the upper wall of my vagina. "Do you want me, sweet Bree?"

"Yes, Jon." These words I can say and they growl low from my throat.

"Tell me," he coaxes gently against my ear as his finger swirls around my clit.

I swallow hard and close my eyes. "I want you inside me."

As soon as the words are out Jon thrust forward, not so gentle this time. I inhale as he fills me completely, my body stretching around the largeness of his cock. I'm pressed against the wall, my nipples diamond-hard against the coolness of the tile.

Jon quickens his movements, pushing further into me until the soft patch of hair at the base of his shaft tickles me with each thrust. I'm wet now and his cock slides easily in and out of my body.

I reach down between my legs and press my body around his length, rewarded with a groan of restrained ecstasy from Jon. I relax into his movements, meeting his thrusts and arcing against his hold on me.

He drives into me fast and hard now, until the line between pleasure and pain blurs to the point of oblivion. Something inside of me clicks and the light inside my darkened world shines brightly. Pain can be a good thing. It tells you when you need to stop and smiles when you can continue. I want it to hurt just enough to know the difference.

And it does.

Little noises – helpless, desperate whimpers of breath rush from my throat each time he pistons himself into my body. He fills me until I think I'll break but he withdraws, and the emptiness has me pushing back, urging him to fill me again. The slick heat of him inside my body intensifies as we move together until I can't tell where his body stops and mine begins.

Jon's breath came in short hot bursts against my neck, my ear, my throat. My body teeters on the edge, the pleasure a pinprick of light in the distance. His movements tighten into controlled measures, and I know he is moments away from letting the wave of the orgasm crash over him. So am I.

Without warning, the pinprick of light explodes behind my vision into a starburst of color and my muscles contract sharply around Jon's thrusting cock. Jon pants sharply as his own release shudders through his, his body connecting solidly with mine then he stills. Inside, each pulse of his cock presses against the inner walls of my pussy as the aftershock of our orgasms ripple outward.

We collapse against the wall, panting as if we'd run a marathon. Jon whispers something in my ear but the pounding of my heart and the churning water drown out the words. Jon's cock slips from my body as he holds me from behind. He wraps both arms around my waist and slides his embrace upward until his forearms cupped the underside of my breasts. I drag my hands from over my head and curl them around his.

We stand there, two bodies cradled in each other, until the water grows tepid. Jon turns off the shower, grabs the towel from behind us and secures it around my body. In one easy motion he sweeps me into his arms and carries me back to the room. He tucks me into the second bed as gently as a newborn babe, then spoons his body around mine. The cocoon warms me. Across the room, Lily's deep, even breathing reaches my ears. I don't think another breath fills my lungs before I slip into the darkness of a dreamless sleep.

AWAKENING
CHAPTER SEVEN

E ven after everything we'd shared, I'll admit I feel a little shy come morning. Lily and Jon stir first. I've never been a morning person and am content to lay quietly and watch them move about the room. Jon's cock stands at attention when he rolls from the bed. Lily's eyes darken as she catches sight of the magnificent erection, kneeling on her bed and motioning him over with a twitch of her finger.

Jon stills like a statue, one leg cocked slightly to the side. He glances over one shoulder, then the other. When his gaze returns to Lily, he presses a finger to his bare chest.

Me? He mouths the word in faux shock and takes a step in her direction.

I can't help but giggle at their play. They'd been together for years and still seem to want each other, but also enjoy each other. They would sit quietly on Lily's bed some afternoons, reading, watching TV, barely speaking a word. It was as natural as their good-natured ribbing or even the occasional disagreement that rocked the walls of the small dorm apartment. Would I ever find that? I wouldn't dare to hope.

Once Jon is within arm's reach, Lily pulls him back to the mattress on her bed and kneels between his legs. She doesn't waste time with any foreplay. Her mouth easily engulfs the long shaft and Jon's mouth falls open to an "o" as her lips surround his dick. She swirls her tongue around the head then dips to take him fully, her lips kissing his body before pulling back. Jon observes her movements, a smile curling along his lips as he strokes her shoulder.

My own body stirs to life watching the action of Lily's cheeks hollowing as she withdraws from Jon's penis. I remain still, eyes partially close wondering if I should look away, but I'm enraptured by the sight of the two of them.

The ridge of muscles in Lily's shoulders and back ripple over the cat-like body – fluid, sure. Her palms knead Jon's thighs, before stealing underneath him to cup his ass and draw him closer to her. He groans and tangles his fingers in her hair, using the grip to control her movements.

Jon looks up and I close my eyes, trying to pretend I'm still asleep. But I can feel the weight of his perusal and a jolt of connection between us zings around my insides.

After a minute, I dare a peek. Jon is fixated on me, a devilish smile playing on his full, sensual lips. His tongue darts out to moisten the bottom lip at the same he extends his hand towards me, beckoning me to join them.

It's tempting but I give my head a little shake. The smile widens. He crooks his index finger and motions to me again, patting the empty space besides him and Lily.

In for a penny, I think, kicking back the sheets tangled around my legs. I rise from the bed, the chill in the room kissing my nipples to life. As I near the bed, Jon pats the spot next to him again, leaning over to support his weight on one elbow. Lily's hand snakes up my leg and grips my ass, all without ever losing the motion of her fellatio on Jon. Gooseflesh did a quick dash around my body.

I sit and Jon positions my body as he wants – my rump near his shoulders, knees pushed up and open wide, baring myself for him. The rush of self-consciousness hits me but recedes quickly.

When he parts the folds with his fingers, heat spirals to my core in anticipation. The breath catches in my throat as his head descends and my heart jumps into my throat when his tongue makes a languid path up my slit.

I rest my weight on my elbows, watching Jon taste and tease the sensitive flesh with his tongue. The fiery center of my desire mushrooms, coursing down my limbs and up my torso. I retreat from the growing wall of desire as it creeps up my neck, fills in the hollows of my cheeks and burns behind my eyes. Not because it's bad but because it's slightly overwhelming in the very best of ways. My consciousness drifts away until it is a separate entity from my body, able to observe with wonder and impartiality.

Jon shifts his body and replaces his tongue with his fingers, slipping one then two into my canal. He curves them upward and the friction against my body elicits a gasp. My need for release coils around my insides ten-fold as he finger-fucks me and I rock my body in rhythm to his movements. Just when I think I will spill over the edge, he withdraws his fingers from my pussy. I growl in frustration.

Jon laughs – the bastard actually laughs – and he traces the wetness spilling down the line of my body with the tip of his finger. He teases the opening of my anus. I tense instinctively and he does nothing else with that finger, but he kisses the inside of my thigh, shushing me until I relax again.

With gentle pressure he inserts his lubed finger into the

tight channel, pushing in and withdrawing until he could add the second finger, scissoring his way slowly into my body. The two drifting halves of my soul crash back together. Pleasure mingles with and overcomes the slight discomfort of the new sensation. Jon works me slowly, probing gently at virgin nerves and untried muscles.

I knew I wouldn't last long. The night's activities left me sensitive and when his mouth again claims my clit I teeter quickly on the brink. Lily bobs a steady rhythm, small moans escaping her now and then between the sucking sounds of her lips around Jon's dick. His cock stands taut, the skin stretched like fine satin over thickly ridged muscle. Lily massages a spot at the base of the head, a particularly sensitive spot seeing how Jon's body contracts in ecstasy and agony if the expression on his face is any indication.

His body arches upward, thrusting deeper into the cavern of Lily's mouth. I feel his gasp of pleasure as he surrounds the center of my sex with his mouth and neither of us can hold back any longer. We shudder and moan our completion and collapse against each other, limbs tangled, breathing in short desperate bursts. My hand finds Jon's caressing Lily's hair and I entwine my fingers with his.

The connection thrumming between us – people who before yesterday I would have called little more than acquaintances – scares me. With them, I see possibilities and contentment. Whatever I am feeling for them is like nothing I'd ever experienced. A tsunami of emotion – quick, unexpected, life altering. That annoying little voice whispers in my head. Maybe it's just sex. My heart answers. Maybe it's more or could be more.

I didn't know what to call the lingering ache that hovers out of my reach, a need I can't explain but need to resolve.

It would be easy to ignore the world and stay naked in their arms for the remainder of the day. The thought crosses my mind a few hundred times. Unfortunately, I'm cursed with an overabundance of responsibility, not to mention two part time jobs through the university.

On Sundays I work in the computer lab from ten to eight. A long day, and not one that pays particularly well, but the lab is usually quiet, and I need to study for an upcoming chemistry mid-term.

After a quick shower, solo this time, I kiss them both good-bye and drag myself and my over-stuffed backpack to the lab. I shush the voice of doubt over whether they care or not that I'm leaving.

I was not used, I remind myself.

At least not in any way that I minded. A blush creeps around my body like a comfortable shawl, warm and wanted.

There are already a few students camped in the hallway waiting on the lab to open. I key in the door code and set up the sign-in sheet on the back table. The students quickly scribble their names, find a seat, and the lab settles into the quiet hum of work. Only the rapid click of keys being struck on the keyboards is heard over the drone of the machines.

I try and concentrate on the text propped against the monitor, but my mind wanders back to the past twelve hours. As the memories play over in my head, my pussy grows damp and pulses at the thought of what could happen next.

Hold up there, I warn myself, reigning in the lustful thoughts. I'd never been one to jump into the deep end of the pool. I'd barely dip my toes into the shallow end without a full recon of the situation. Now I was not only swimming in the deep end, but I'd also dived headfirst from the high diving board.

My psych class filled in answers. College really could be a pain in the ass, but it also replaces therapy when you take the right course load.

I'd grown up with an aunt and uncle after my parents died. An only child. Orphaned. I'd barely known my dad's brother and his wife when they were saddled with the sad and lonely seven-year-old delivered to their door. Childless by choice, they sought to control every move and thought I made to make their lives easier.

I'd been desperate for love and security, having had the first and lost the second. They could provide neither. Surrounded by their conditional affections, I learned to be skeptical about love and rely on myself for whatever security I needed. I never expected to find it, which made life lonely but predictably secure.

Security does not replace love.

After just a few hours, I find myself wanting what had been missing the last sixteen years. It's ridiculous, I tell myself. Two people cannot replace sixteen years of absence in one short evening.

A text dings on my phone. It's from Lily and my heart does a skip-jump. I open the message.

I can still smell you on my sheets, taste you on my skin. Eager for seconds.

And just like that, my breath is ragged, my pulse is racing. A thousand thoughts ping pong around inside my head but there's really only one that matters.

Yes.

To whatever happens. I don't know why I'm so sure all of a sudden but I am.

I think about what I know of Lily and realize it's damn

little. We'd be paired through the Dean of Students' Office, both older students living among mostly teenagers. I'd been in my second year at the time; she in her third. I'd doubled up some courses in the summer sessions while she traveled abroad. Now we were both set to graduate at the end of the semester.

She's the New York bohemian to my displaced Southern Belle. It wasn't long after we moved in together that Lily introduced me to Jon and by Christmas they spent as many nights at our place as they did his place off campus.

We made the usual chit chat, but it was innocuous though sometimes flirtatious and I never gave it a second thought. Remember, I'm Switzerland. It didn't occur to me that it meant any more than idle banter.

She and Jon both had a good sense of humor that complimented my own and while we were far from friends, it was nice to have someone to wave hello in the cafeteria or while walking across campus.

I'd known since junior high I was attracted to both girls and boys but didn't know what to make of it. I kept my head down in the locker room during gym class for fear that my eyes would give me away.

The internet being the greatest teacher of all things unknown, I learned the word *bisexual* and read other curious stories of trysts that got my young mind working. I had no one to ask. No one to confide in.

So, like all good southern belles I kept it to myself.

My previous sexual experience left me certain that something in me was broken or seriously off kilter. How could I be normal if sex left me feeling more unsatisfied than before? I avoided relationships that might lead to something more.

And now all I want to do is live out more of the fantasy stories I'd read in secret in my bed late at night.

I groan inwardly as my body betrays the inner workings of my mind. I'd gone without a bra tonight – the chilly temps in the computer lab kept me in a sweatshirt most evenings – and my nipples pebble beneath the heavy cotton.

Just by moving my shoulders I can caress the hardened nubs with the course material and the friction alone has me squirming in my chair. I sigh forlornly at the clock. Seven hours left on my shift. I groan but when heads swivel, I quickly cover with a cough and bury my head back in my organic chem book.

When it's finally time to close the computer lab I practically dance through the room making sure all the desktops are powered down. Snatching up my book bag I hurry through the empty hallways, cutting through the science building back to the dorm.

The lobby is filled to overflowing. Students returning from the weekend. Pizza delivery drivers. There's a low hum of activity throughout the dorm on normal days but on a Sunday the place resembles Times Square on New Year's Eve.

I've never thought of myself as part of the college crowd. Maybe it's because of my age. I feel far removed from the carefree attitudes of my fellow students.

Mostly I envy them the circle of friends, the presence of family dropping them off or helping them move in and out of the dorm. I want a family to call my own.

But more importantly, a family that calls me one of their own. I don't ever want to be the unwanted orphan again.

And I don't want to be the third wheel.

I skirt the crowd, quickly check the front desk for any messages and take the steps to my third-floor room two at a time.

I try the door and find it locked, ignoring the stab of disappointment as I slide my key into the lock. I'm hoping Lily and Jon are just smarter than I was last night, locking the door to intrusion as they fool around. The room is empty and against all efforts my eyes burn with the threat of tears.

What did you think? I scold myself, dropping my purse on the unmade bed. *They'd be waiting to fulfill all your fantasies?* The tangle of sheets and covers remind me of our bodies wrapped around each other just a few hours earlier.

I plop on the bed, depression settling across my shoulders. How fast I'd started to want something, I admit to myself. I hoped they'd still be around, still interested...but it didn't matter, I try to convince myself as I pull the backpack on my bed. The weight in my gut is a reminder: I'm alone.

It's then that I see the piece of paper fashioned into a rose by the pillow. A whiff of Lily's perfume meets me when I pick it up and hold the rose beneath my nose. The heady fragrance wafts through my senses and entwines with the memories from the previous evening. Things low in my body tighten and heat coils along the muscles of my sex. I open the folded paper.

I know you're disappointed to find the room empty but it's no more disappointed than Jon and I feel at not being there.

I know that will be hard for you to believe.

If you can find it in yourself to trust us, sweet Bree, Jon and I have many surprises in store for you.

Last night was a beginning.

An elaborate 'L' is scrawled along the bottom with a lip

imprint in a shade I recognize as Lily's. I read the note two or three more times, certain I'm reading it wrong.

Jon and I.

The words echo in my head and something like hope flutters in the pit of my stomach.

WAITING
CHAPTER EIGHT

CHAPTER EIGHT

The week crawls by more slowly than I ever imagine possible. On top of everything else, we are coming up on a four-day weekend for fall break, so my edginess is mirrored to some degree by the other students. The campus will be mostly empty for the holiday, and I can't help but think back to last weekend.

I find little notes from Lily or Jon everywhere I go: the shower, the café, my classes, the coffee shop, the computer lab. Quiet reminders they have not forgotten me.

I guess they know me better than I realize.

The notes are playful, sexy, romantic, serious. How they're managing to hide them without being seen or someone else finding them, I have no idea.

By Wednesday I'm ready to scream. When Thursday finally rolls into Friday the weight lifts from my shoulders.

I'm working in the library stacks Friday afternoon when Lily shows up. A long-sleeved black sheath dress moves over her body, the clingy material riding her curves like a dirty thought. My dirty thoughts, to be exact.

I salivate over the pair of knee-high boots encasing the long, luscious legs. A flush creeps up my face watching her saunter my way.

"Hiya, professor." She pecks a friendly kiss on my cheek.

My heart plummets into my stomach with the sisterly gesture. Despite the many notes telling me otherwise, maybe last weekend was just a diversion for them.

I smile in spite of the ache carving my heart out of my chest. "Hey there, Lily."

She reads my disappointment and cups my chin with her palm, lifting my face. I can't meet her gaze at first, but she waits until I do.

"I'm sorry. I didn't want you to feel any pressure. Jon and I wanted to give you time away from us." She does a side-to-side motion with her head, as if weighing her words. "In case you're having some regrets."

I shrug and push the glasses up my nose. "I have no regrets about last weekend." Unspoken words hang on the end of my sentence.

She regards me beneath hooded eyes. "But...?"

I start to shrug again but stop myself. "You guys disappeared. I wasn't sure what to think. Even with all the notes."

Lily rests her forehead against my own, lowers her mouth to mine and brushes a gentle yet possessive kiss on my lips. The hollowness in my gut fills with longing and my body clenches in search of something to fill the emptiness.

"Come." Lily takes me by the hand and leads me deeper into the stacks. Desks are intermixed with the shelves, and we select one near the back left corner.

She pats the tabletop and I hop up. Lily stands close, the aroma of orchids swirling about her.

"I wanted you to have time to think without our libidos in the way. You're not put off by what happened between the three of us?"

"No," I gasp, surprised at the question. "I enjoyed it." I blush at the admission, however and Lily traces the curve of my jawline with her index finger.

"Sweet, Bree." Her caramel eyes darkened to mocha, the pupils constricting to pinpricks. I see my own reflection in the golden orbs. "Jon said you would. He's had his eye on you since that first semester."

"Jon noticed me?" The thought of Jon, or anyone for that matter, noticing me is strangely wonderful.

I've always been invisible, mostly by choice, preferring to be ignored than risk putting myself out there and be hurt again. But the loneliness overpowered me at times.

Lily strokes her thumb down the line of my face then cups my chin. "A person would have to be half-blind and completely stupid not to notice you. You're intelligent, funny, witty, honest." Lily presses closer, nudging my knees open with her hip. Her left-hand rests provocatively between my open thighs. "And then there's your ass and your mouth," Lily follows the bow of my upper lip with the tip of her middle finger. A staccato rhythm pounds deep in my sex. "We've had long discussions about your mouth."

I swallow the lump thrumming in my throat and resist the urge to wet my lips. "I don't understand though. If you and Jon are together then...?" I let the thought trail off. I want an answer but not enough to ask the question, afraid of the answer. What am I to them?

"We have an open relationship, each pursuing other people as we want. We've always wanted to find someone that we would share but no one ever interested us both. Until now."

Lily inches her left hand forward, teasing the flesh of my inner thigh with a light stroke. Instinct opens my legs. I want her touch. A deeper instinct, however, shadows my desire for uninhibited release. It isn't just the caress of a lover or lovers that I desire. It's for someone to take control and lead me, tell me what I want is okay regardless of its darkness. In that darkness I search for the light of being my true self. I didn't want to lose myself to the submission.

I want to find myself.

"Lily, I..." So many emotions, so few words suitable to tell her I want her. I want her. I want Jon. The merest thought of what we shared Saturday night brings a rush of liquid fire to the center of my belly.

But I didn't have the words to voice the desire zinging through my system or the experience to express those desires through the hands of a lover. I search her eyes for guidance.

As I hoped, she read my uncertainty. "It's ok, Bree. We can teach you to trust what you're feeling."

Lily's fingers press on the cotton of my panties, and I shut my eyes as I wait for her to breach the barrier and delve her skillful fingers into my flesh. My breathing echoes in my ears and the beat of my heart pulses at the back of my throat and in places much lower in my body.

"Look at me, Gabrielle," she demands softly, and I open my eyes instantly. "You have to learn to trust us as you have trusted no other."

Trust. I hate the fucking word. For something so wonderful it leads mostly to pain.

"I'm not sure I know how." The admission, barely audible to even me, weighs heavy between us.

"First you must learn to trust yourself." Lily takes my right hand and guides it to where her fingers stroke my panties against the cotton. "If I told you to take off your panties right now, would you?"

Lost in the dark desire of her eyes, I can't answer. I steal a glance over her shoulder at the corridor leading into the stacks. It's empty but at any moment someone could walk in and see me. See us.

Lily presses our fingers more firmly against my panties, the dampness from my desire soaking the material in warmth. "If I told you to touch yourself like you were when we found you that night, to stroke and please yourself...if I told you I would not laugh or judge you or be embarrassed, that I would only find pleasure as you brought yourself to orgasm while I watched, could you believe me?"

My mouth and throat are bone dry. I swallow hard, but she doesn't stop.

"If I asked you to give me total control," she brings both my hands to the side of my body and holds them lightly beneath hers, much like Jon had tried to do in the shower. My heart hammers in my chest and my fear screams at me to pull away, but at the same time my sex clenches in pulsing arousal, wanting more.

Much more.

Lily leans in close and moves one hand beneath my shirt and drags the cotton of the bra down until my breast spills over the fabric. She palms the flesh, grazing the nipple with her fingers. With the other hand she returns to my open legs, this time drawing her finger down the edge of my panties, skimming lightly where the fabric meets flesh. I breathe in shallow, urgent pants.

"Would you trust me to push you to the edge, then catch you if you fall?"

There'd never been anyone to catch me. I'd always been the only one I could count on. Of course, I'd never let anyone get close enough to find out if I could put my trust in them, always certain they would let me down.

My certainty doesn't quite have the weight it had before. The night with Lily and Jon pushed everything I was, everything I knew about myself. And they were offering me more.

Do I possess the courage to test these boundaries, to explore this dangerous and exciting world Lily hints at?

I start to lift my hand to join hers but Lily murmurs low in her throat, "Don't move your hands, Gabrielle." When I return my hands to my side, she slips the elastic of my panties aside and teases the outer walls of my pussy.

"Jon likes pussy," she smiles mischievously and strokes her finger lightly through my curls. She slides two fingers into my channel, fucking me with a slow, agonizing rhythm. I hover on the edge of orgasm almost instantly, so close I feel the flutter of muscles deep inside my body clench in anticipation of the release Lily's fingers' promise.

"But he really gets hard for anal." She pushes her other hand beneath my rump to the cleft of my cheeks, then teases the ring of muscle there. There'd been fantasies... dark fantasies I would scarcely admit to myself.

Her breath caresses my face, her voice throaty and deep as it rumbles in my ear while her fingers play havoc on my body. "For him, it's the ultimate trust that a lover can give."

She intensifies the in and out of her fingers and when I crash over the sweet precipice just seconds later, she swallows my moans beneath a crushing kiss. Lily takes the fingers that just moments ago plied my eager body and slips them between our joined lips. The tangy taste mingles on our kiss, and she quickly licks away the flavor of my orgasm.

Could I give that trust to Jon? To her? Did I have it in me to give myself over to Lily and Jon? What if they betray me like everyone else? But they'd had all week to betray me – to tell everyone what we'd done, and they hadn't. Maybe it is time to trust someone. Especially myself.

"I want to trust myself. I want to trust you and Jon."

My leap of faith is rewarded instantly. The smile explodes in her eyes before she rests her forehead against mine. Her breath escapes slowly and her shoulders drop.

"Thank you." She presses a sweet, chaste kiss to my cheek. "I will not let you down. I swear it. I know you don't believe it yet, but I will work to prove it true every day we are together."

The entirety of her promise sinks in like water to the parched ground. She speaks the words with such sincerity, but they are not a balm to my wounded heart.

They are a vice.

Lily pulls back and draws a silver chain from around her neck and lays the items dangling from the end in her palm. Three keys elaborately decorated with what I think are hieroglyphics along the shaft and head. The irony does not escape me.

That mysterious, challenging smile returns to Lily's full, rose lips. "Do you remember the story of Ebeneezer Scrooge, how three ghosts visited him, each with something different to teach?"

A shiver tingles down my spine, skittering along the edge of my soul. Sarcasm singsongs in my voice. "The ghosts of Christmas past, present and future are going to visit me?"

She laughs, a sound deep and throaty that excites me. "Not exactly."

Lily removes the chain and slips it over my head, then drops the keys beneath the collar of my shirt. The cool silver nestles between the valley of my breasts.

"Listen carefully Bree. You will not see me again until this weekend is over. But Jon or I will always be near. I swear it."

My senses go on alert. I want Lily and Jon to be my teachers in this adventure. Would they give me to someone else?

Trust, I remind myself. And I want this like I'd wanted nothing else since I was seven. The prospect of the adventure alone is enough to curb my disappointment and concern.

"You will be visited by three spirits." That smile returns. I shiver as she presses her hand over the slight rise of the keys by my shirt. "Each will have a key to your..." She hesitates, looking to the heavens as if to pluck the word from the sky. She finally concludes with "Education. Trust them as you would trust me or Jon – they are friends we trust completely, and we chose them for you. Remember this," She rests her index finger on the outline of the three keys snuggled between my breasts. "You hold the key. Say my name and the lessons will be over."

Over? My body tenses. Did they only want to be with me if I could pass their little test? I'd grown up trying to earn love and swore to myself I'd never play anyone's games again when it came to love.

Quick to read the body language screaming my worry, Lily wraps her hand around the back of my neck and draws me closer to her. "Not us, Bree. We won't be over." She moves her hand between us, touching her heart then mine.

"Jon and I want to be with you and until you tell us otherwise, we will be. I only mean that the lessons we've designed will be over. This is meant to test you, yes. But it'll be fun as shit. I think you'll like what happens. I think you will want what happens. Enjoy yourself." She squeezes the back of my neck and playfully nips my nose. "But mostly it's to teach that you can trust yourself and us. Do you understand?"

"I understand but what will…"

She silences my words beneath her fingers. "No questions, Bree. That is part of the lesson. You must trust us completely. I promise you this: beyond some wear and tear on your pride or ego, you will not be physically injured. But you will be tested. This will challenge you, maybe even reveal some parts of yourself you didn't know existed or thought long buried or forgotten. Are you up for it?"

I want to ask what three *ghosts* could teach me that she and Jon could not. A thousand questions ping-ponged around my head. The coolness of the three keys kissed my left breast.

However uncertain, I replied, "Yes."

Her shoulders dropped; relief evident in her face. Could she be nervous about this? About me?

"That's my girl. Tonight, be ready at ten. We will see you soon, sweetness."

Lily captures my mouth in a deep, probing kiss then turns and disappears into the stacks.

The questions rip around my brain and a delicious warmth coils around my insides. What had I gotten myself into? I press my fingers to my temples, lost in the vortex of desire, confusion, excitement and anxiety. I caught the scent of my recent orgasm on my fingers and inhaled the fragrance, the sweet tangy mixture so familiar and so unfamiliar at the same time.

I checked my watch. Three o'clock. I got off work at seven. Then three hours to prepare for...what?

For my first day of school.

LESSONS
BOOK TWO

MASTERED BY DEGREES

Lessons

METAMORPHOSIS
CHAPTER ONE

The steam mists over my body as I stand beneath the cascade of water, letting my anxiety swirl down the drain with the water. The memory of Jon and Lily's attentions last weekend hovers at the front of my memory.

How did I go from a near virginal twenty-four-year-old to ménage à trois in a single night?

I'm not sure I care about the answer too much. The fact is, it happened.

Lily's kiss. Jon's touch.

Just the memory is enough to send a shiver zip lining around my body. The shiver is equal parts anticipation and insecurity. When I was with them, it felt right. When they are away, it's so easy to question everything about our time together.

I long for their hands to brush away my fears.

But they don't appear.

This is meant to test you.

You must trust us completely.

I don't know that I've ever trusted anyone completely.

Not even myself.

I go through the motions of washing my hair, shaving my legs, soaping my body in a daze. My brain constantly shifts back to the previous weekend. Lily's first touch. Jon's lusty appraisal. These memories physically manifest on my body: gooseflesh, smiles, a tightness as the muscles remember want and release.

From friendly roommates to lovers in a single night. Potential hovered over the relationship now, especially with Lily's proposal in the library.

Would you trust me to push you to the edge, then catch you if you fall?

What did she mean? What did she and Jon have in store for me? I guess tonight we'll see if my bravery in that moment will be confirmed or wash away like the water down the drain.

The mystery of the three ghosts - three lessons - appeals to the scientist in me. I want to know what Lily will teach me. I hope to be as good a student for her and Jon as I have been for my professors.

Back in the room, the loneliness is tangible. Lily's side of the room is oddly quiet, and not the kind of quiet I am used to when she spends her evenings and weekends with Jon. I curl up on her bed, wrap myself in the memory of her perfume still lingering on the sheets. Orchids on fresh linen. The room feels strange now. How can a week change my life so drastically?

I'd been alone most of my twenty-four years, even when I was living with my aunt and uncle. In the beginning, I begged for their love and acceptance through perfection: perfectly tidy room, perfect grades, perfect manners. It was never enough and I soon learned that nothing ever would be enough. After high school, I took off and set out on my own until I could access my trust fund at eighteen. They tried to control me even then and another four years of lawyers and courts and bullshit kept me from starting my life.

But on my own, I discovered a new loneliness. The emptiness of a crowded room, the void in my heart. I'd denied my need for love for so long I'd begun to believe I didn't need it or anyone. I know...so jaded at twenty-four.

In less than one week, Lily and Jon wedged a crack in the carefully constructed wall around my heart.

And ignited a passion deeper than I ever dreamed possible.

But they also made me aware of the true depth of my loneliness. I didn't want to be lonely anymore. I just didn't know if I could change.

I open the closet door to select an outfit and find a surprise. A sleek white dress about two sizes too small for my size twelve frame. I run my hand down the front of the dress and turn it around to view the back only to get another surprise.

There isn't one.

Or at least not much of one. The two shoulder sections are secured by a slim silver chain. The dress tapers down to the hips where it ends in an almost embarrassingly nonexistent hem.

So much for wearing panties and a bra but the conventional undergarments go against the *spirit* of the evening. I laugh at my Ebenezer joke. I told you my sense of humor is a little under the radar.

If I am going to lose my inhibitions, I might as well start with my panties.

I slip on the dress and stare in the mirror and try to see myself as others might. My hair is a dark brownish-auburn, straight with a slight upturn at the ends. I have to admit I like my eyes. They're the color of my birthstone, peridot – a little ghostly if I'm being honest but unique.

Some long-forgotten ancestor gifted me with excellent bone structure in the form of high cheekbones and good birthing hips. Mountains and valleys of flesh and bone. I'm no lithe runway model though. There are curves in those hills.

Passable is the word that comes to mind, even though I still see myself as Switzerland. I can see the benefits of my hours in the pool and on my bike even though my tummy rounds outward slightly no matter how many crunches I force on myself.

I could probably stand to lose a few pounds, but the weight is more muscle. My doctor doesn't agree. Fuck the old bastard.

Anyone looking would probably say my breasts are just right, enough for a handful, not overly large. My waist and hips are all woman, full and curvy. My legs are my best feature, in my opinion; long and tapered, with well-muscled thighs and calves. They seem to take up half of my five eight frame.

The dark areolas are visible beneath the white dress, as is the triangle of hair at the juncture of my thighs, but only in bright light luckily. I don't think there is much danger of them being seen at this time of night.

The dress tucks in at my waist and compliments my curves. A simple pair of pumps complete the outfit. I let my hair fall freely, tucking one side behind my ear.

Finally, I slip the chain over my head and nestle the three keys between my breasts. The weight is a talisman: a reminder of Lily and Jon and their promise.

At ten a knock sounds on my door and I open it to find the most incredibly beautiful man I've ever seen. When I remember to breathe, I give him a once over because, why not?

California chic: blonde, muscled, tan. I could easily see him in a dive suit carrying a surfboard. He wears a chauffeur's uniform, the cap tucked neatly under one well shaped bicep.

I snap my gaping mouth shut but other body parts contract involuntarily and I immediately question the wisdom of going out this evening with no panties.

"Ms. Gabrielle Fontenot." He extends his right arm, which I accept, in awe of the muscles flexing beneath my fingers.

Broad shoulders fill out the neatly tailored jacket, accentuating a trim waist and thick legs. Beside his commanding presence – he stood nearly a half foot taller than me – I feel diminutive, feminine.

But also, unsure.

As we walk through the dorm, a few people lingering in the hall stop and stare openly, a situation I normally find uncomfortable. I don't like being the center of attention.

"Jon was right," Mr. California whispers, securing my hand between his forearm and his left hand. "You are quite captivating."

I manage not to snort my disbelief. "That's kind but I hardly think they are staring at me."

"Look at their eyes. They may start on me, but they linger on you."

Wow. There may be women not swayed by that kind of flattery, but I'm not one of them. My first reaction is denial. My second reaction is denial.

Finally, I go with, "Thank you." It's all I can really think of to say.

Whether it's my handsome escort's compliment or the

dress or some mystical power of the talisman hovering at the valley of my breasts, I revel in the attention now, cocking my head slightly and putting a little extra swagger in my walk.

Who am I?

Let's go find out.

RULES
CHAPTER TWO

Outside the cool air slides across my bare skin. My nipples harden in response to the intimate caress; there's very little barrier to keep out the chill. The October breeze swirls the newly fallen leaves from the sidewalk as if clearing a path to the waiting limousine.

While I didn't expect a pumpkin coach with footman and four magnificent stallions, I also didn't expect the black stretch Mercedes parked with...well, one magnificent stallion.

I'd barely finished the thought when the passenger side door opens and a pair of long legs unfurl from the back seat.

Two magnificent stallions, I amend the earlier thought as those long legs unfurl into a body made for sexy tv commercials. *Holy shit*. He's the RideShare driver that took us downtown. Jacob.

He is darkness in every regard, from the ebony hair, unreflecting eyes, and fiercely brooding demeanor. He is midnight to Mr. California's sun. We stand toe to toe – my eyes only reach his chin - and he waits, as if looking for a cue I will go forward with the evening or run and hide back in the dorm.

"I shaved my legs," I blurt out before my internal filter can stop me. "And I have a killer dress to show them off. Let's party."

Did I mention my sense of humor?

Mr. California bursts out laughing and Jacob echoes the sound.

"My lady," he opens the car door and sweeps his hand inside with a grand gesture. I step into the dimly lit interior, wondering what other surprises await me this evening.

The rich leather interior is nothing I've ever experienced. Soft and supple, it caresses my bare legs as I slide onto the seat. Up front, a tinted glass separates the rear compartment from the front seat.

The door closes as Jacob settles onto the seat with me. He regards me beneath hooded eyes, the smoldering gaze fanning the embers started from his gaze during our first trip together. Did he know who I was then? Did he know about tonight?

The car pulls away from the curb and we disappear into the streets of the city, but the questions don't disappear so readily.

"Good evening, Gabrielle. May I kiss you?"

My eyes widen at the request, but I nod.

He cradles my face in his palms and brushes a feather soft kiss to my lips. "I'm Jacob."

"I remember." Because I do. A girl needs a name to call out even in her fantasies.

"The less handsome but hulking behemoth driving us tonight is Dylan."

The audible click of an intercom sounds followed quickly by a deep voice. "Bite me, Jacob."

Jacob laughs. "I already did that, my love."

Click. "Did I thank you for that?"

"No. Now shut up and drive."

"Yes, sir," comes the smart-assed reply, followed by, "Besides, my turn is coming."

Jacob's attention returns to me, distracting me before I can ask what Dylan's comment means. He follows the outline of the chain around my neck until his finger rests on the three keys.

His knuckles graze my left nipple as he releases the chain but it's not until his fingers skim over my ribs that I tense slightly.

He withdraws his hand, letting it fall to his thigh. "Sorry. Ticklish?"

"Very." My uncle used to hold me down under the guise of *play* and dig his fingers into my ribs until I cried. He thought it was funny. Me? Not so much.

"Then this is the perfect segue. Do you remember your safeword?"

"Safe word?"

"Yes. Anytime throughout the night, just say Lily's name and the evening ends. No hard feelings."

Click. "We both know you're already hard, dear."

Jacob smiles and caresses the side of my exposed leg with his thumb, stopping at the hem. Twenty-four hours ago, I would have kneed Jacob in the crotch. I am thinking about his crotch all right. It's amazing what twenty-four hours can do.

"Jacob." My voice quivers and I swallow the apprehension knotted in my throat. I want to sound casual but even to me my voice is breathless and eager. "Jacob as in Jacob Marley?" I ask as his thumb traces the line where my dress ends. "Really?"

The laugh that flows from his throat is guttural and seductive, a rumbling baritone that fills the confines of the car. "Lily said you were smart. But no, the Jacob is a coincidence."

"Are you my first spirit?"

"Not exactly." Jacob sidles up closer, leaning forward. His palm covers my thigh now. He nuzzles my ear, his tongue flicking along the sensitive curve of the lobe.

A current of electricity rushes through my body but I situate my hand on his very broad chest and push him back. "Exactly what are you then?" I practically hum the words.

He sits back against the seat, his hand moving to rest casually on my knee. "I am your gatekeeper. A protector of sorts. My job is to make sure you arrive safely to your destination each night, and safely home afterward."

My eyes widen and I inhale sharply. My thoughts race back to the day outside the Saenger Theater downtown, watching Lily and Jon walk away hand in hand. I'd wanted a protector.

"Why do I need a protector?" Doubt wiggles its way between the lust and curiosity tonight has awakened. Maybe I'm in over my head. A minor-league player in a field of experienced professionals.

"It was Jon's request. He's quite taken with you and doesn't want your experience to be anything but ..." Jacob retraces a path from my knee to the very top of my thigh. Liquid fire shoots to my core and the blood pulses quicker in my veins. "Pleasurable. He wanted someone neutral who could assess if your physical well-being is at risk or determine if there's any mental distress. I'm to call a stop to the night if I sense either."

The mention of Jon's name eases the tension winding

its way through my system and Lily's words echo in my ears.

You will not see me again until this weekend is over. But either Jon or I will always be near. I swear it.

I incline my head to the tinted glass hiding Dylan. "Is Lily or Jon in the front seat with Dylan?"

Jacob smiles devilishly. "Lily and Jon can be trusted."

Not an admission but I take it as one and tamp the nerves down. I am determined to enjoy their hard work.

"They asked me to give you this. It's a list of rules for your time with us."

Rules. Flashes of my childhood play like a bad movie and raises the tiny hairs at the back of my neck. He hands me an expensive envelope, linen if I'm to guess by the feel of it.

Jacob clicks on an overhead light so I can see. A familiar "L" is embossed in gold filigree on the back flap and I withdraw an equally expensive piece of stationary. It matches the first note left for me after my night Jon and Lily.

The note reads simply:

Rule 1. You're in charge.

Rule 2. If in doubt, see Rule 1.

I fold the note and stuff it back in the envelope, absorbing the power of the words.

"Are the rules something you can live with?" Jacob asks, accepting the envelope and placing it between two crystal glasses on the small side table.

"Did you read the note?" I incline my head toward the envelope.

I sink a little lower in the seat, crossing my legs and angling my body toward Jacob. He maneuvers his body so we are practically entwined. My thigh rubs the front of his trousers and the hardness beneath the fabric brands my flesh.

But I don't pull away.

A quick shake of his head sends a section of dark hair angling across his forehead. "I wasn't given permission to read the note. No one said I couldn't ask, however."

I'd be lying to say I'm not intrigued by his answer. "Do you always follow the rules?"

"Only where Lily is concerned."

"But not Jon?

His husky laugh goes straight to my pussy, an intimate sound in the confines of the limo. He avoids the question.

"I see why Jon and Lily are so taken with you."

Curiosity overtakes my natural hesitation. "Why is that?"

"Outside of being very beautiful," he holds up his hand as I open my mouth to protest. "Don't disagree because you won't or don't see it. I can't be the first to tell you this, not even the first tonight. But..."

Jacob gives a little sweeping motion with his hand, as if to brush away my opposition.

"The fact that you truly don't yet see your beauty, makes your appeal very...appealing."

He claims what little space remains between us, the woodsy aroma of his aftershave swirls with something spicy and I lean closer.

"I'd like very much to kiss you again."

The bold admission takes me by surprise and as he pushes me back into the leather seat with the closeness of his body, I see the dark desire slide across his eyes.

When I don't object, he kisses me, a taste only, moving his lips over mine slow and deliberate. He guides my hand to the front of his trousers, covering the swell of his cock with my hand. His flesh leaps beneath my touch and Jacob sucks in a sharp breath.

"So deliciously sweet."

He expertly snakes a hand beneath my thighs but goes no further. The swell of his cock brands my palm and the ache between my legs swells.

I moan and gasp, curling my fingers into the lapel of his jacket.

I'm holding on, trying to center myself in the here and now. I don't recognize myself. Am I someone new? Or is this who I always was?

His hand urges my knees further apart and Jacob cups the back of my legs, drawing my thigh upward so my leg wraps around his waist.

He presses forward, grinding against the bare flesh between my thighs when Dylan's disembodied voice announces, "We're here, Jacob."

EDGE
CHAPTER THREE

No! I'm not there yet.

Jacob ceases his explorations and pulls back slightly. My body hums the Halleluiah chorus of need, my breath ragged. I whimper. Jacob grins and smothers my lips with his.

"I wish we had more time, Gabrielle. Perhaps later, if you're not too tired."

"I think I'd have to be dead to be too tired for you."

Jacob laughs and I blush head to toe. He adjusts his trousers and looks out the window, giving me a moment to straighten my dress and compose myself, although no amount of time would erase the kiss-swollen lips or warm blush on my cheeks. "I'm ready."

He glances back over his shoulder and winks. "Lily and Jon will be around even if you can't see them. Remember the safeword. And have fun. Jon and Lily have chosen well for you. Trust them. And yourself."

Jacob opens the door and steps out of the limo, extending his hand back to me. I slip my hand into his, the point of contact warm and secure. The same cannot be said for our location, however.

We hadn't been driving long, or my recollection is fuzzy from lust, but we seem a world away from school and New Orleans proper. Though I can see the elevated span of I-10 in the distance, not even the lights of the city make a dent in the night. If it weren't for the streetlamps along the long driveway, we'd be swallowed by darkness.

I slowly pivot my head, taking in the immense house looming before us. Only *house* doesn't quite fit the structure. Mansion. The place is a mansion. The stone exterior is accented in places by a dark rich wood and there are more arches than even Ronald McDonald could count.

But more impressive than the house is the surrounding landscape...and its vast emptiness. I didn't pay attention on the drive over, my mind occupied elsewhere, but I didn't think we'd been on the road long enough to escape civilization so thoroughly.

The house sits at the valley of two sloping sections of land, the earth wrapping around the foundation like a woolen scarf. The tail of the scarf juts out into the water to float away on the soft lap of waves and moonglow. Not a single window in the three-story structure reveals a light within.

Jacob tugs on my hand and I fall in step beside him. We descend the winding path to the house, moving between the manicured lawn and sculpted boxwoods. As we start up the stairs the front door swings open and serves up an Asian woman, her midnight hair falling in perfect ringlets over her shoulders. She greets us with a half-smile.

Behind her, a grand staircase frames her body in swirls of ivory marble and wrought iron. The banister splits right and left, the curve of iron giving the illusion of black wings. Appropriate for our hostess.

She wears black, from the lacy sheath dress to the four-inch spike fuck-me-pumps. She looks me up and down and I suddenly know how the last box of Girl Scout cookies must feel.

Jacob steps aside and propels me forward with a touch at the small of my back. When he releases my hand, I stop and turn to him, the question on my lips apparently obvious.

"This is as far as I go, Bree." He silences my protests with two fingers to my lips, then kisses me gently. His tongue teases mine briefly, leaving me breathless, aware of every nerve between my mouth and sex. "We'll be near enough, and you will be safe. I promise."

More promises of my safety and urging to trust. This is the theme of my interaction with Jon and Lily.

That untrusting little voice in my head whispers, 'Yeah, right' but I nod anyway and allow Jacob to retreat. I return my attention to the door.

What have I gotten myself into?

"Hello," I croak, my throat suddenly dry as day old toast. I try and ignore the patter of nerves clawing at my stomach by clenching my fists. I clear the hoarseness from my throat and try again. "I'm Bree."

The woman turns without a word and is devoured by the house. So much for her hostess-of-the-year award.

I swallow the pissy sarcasm. *Guess I'll get the door.* OK. I don't swallow *all* the pissy sarcasm. I push the door closed, letting it hit with more force than necessary.

I collapse against the door, let my anger trickle away, but it's replaced by a sense of unease as the echo of the door hitting the jam ripples into the cavernous home and disappears.

What am I doing here? Am I disappearing as well by being here tonight? Lily and Jon's faces float behind my eyes when I close them. It's odd. I feel like I've known them forever. Rather than sex complicating my feelings for them, it simplifies it.

How can they feel safe? When nothing in my life has ever felt right, they do. When no one in my life ever felt like they'd make room for me, they've made *three* feel like the absolutely perfect number. I can't explain it. With Jon and Lily, I feel like I can finally be the person I was meant to be.

The question is: can I let myself be that person?

My hostess is disappearing down a hall, her reed thin body undulating, each step radiating sexual confidence. I fall in step behind her but I don't even pretend to myself that I walk with the same grace.

Will I be able to walk with the same air after my education is complete?

Probably not, I laugh to myself. That kind of attitude comes from years of practice...and reinforcement.

She weaves her way through the house, the methodic tapping of her black heels on the hardwood floors unhurried, hypnotic. The sound echoes softly against the twelve-foot ceiling, even that too boisterous a noise in the stark civility of the open space around us.

The interior is simple but refined: sharp, clean lines. Neutral colors. The art work is what makes it truly amazing however. In just the first few minutes I see pieces by Andy Warhol, Alma Thomas, Kandinsky.

The art is priceless but my attention is drawn back to the woman before me. I drag my eyes up the seam of her stockings until it disappears beneath the ridiculously short hem of the dress. Bell sleeves swish against her wrists and thighs.

The peek-a-boo lace outfit hides everything and nothing. She's braless. Pantiless. But you really can't see any more than snippets of skin slightly lighter or darker in color than her dress.

But what's really stealing the attention is the collar around her neck, a leash falling down the line of her spine. A silver lock dangles on the side of the collar, the only break in the monochromatic color scheme of her wardrobe.

Who's waiting in the wings with a key? What does it even mean? I press my fingertips over the three keys I wear. What will these unlock for me? Or are they to lock me in?

After a maze of turns she disappears around a corner. I follow and nearly collide with the man standing just beneath the massive archway.

REFLECTION
CHAPTER FOUR

I jump back slightly, drawing a quick breath. The blood rushes from my face to pool in the balls of my feet.

I give him a quick once over. Slightly crooked nose. Prominent jaw. He's solid based on my collision with him. But that's not the predominant characteristic.

He absorbs the space around us, not just with his presence, but with the look in his eyes. Which he was using to look down on me. Not because he was arrogant. Or, well, not only because he was arrogant. He was just that tall.

"Good evening, Gabrielle. Welcome. I'm Dominick. I'm glad to see our guest of honor has arrived. Please join us."

Guest of honor? Us?

My eyes dart around the room, landing briefly on the other two faces in the background; a gentleman stands to the right, a woman is seated to my left.

The woman who escorted me from the door pulls out the chair at one end of an elaborately set table and waits. Still silent. That's a bit annoying by now. Does she speak?

It's on the tip of my tongue to question my place as the

guest of honor but Dominick takes my hand and tucks it in the crook of his arm, holding it in place with the weight of the other hand which consumes mine. The pressure of his fingers, light but unyielding, do not allow the option of removing my hand.

They seem to steal my voice as well.

My mind tumbles as Dominick leads me to the table. Candles flicker on all sides of the room, on every surface. Shadows dance on the wall, and I can see my own altered perception in the distorted images. My reality is changing and shifting, a mingling of both darkness and light.

I sit and the chair engulfs me, the velvet cushions caressing me intimately. Another theme for the night. Swallowed by the darkness. Devoured by the house. Consumed by my host's hands.

I looked at the table. Was I on the menu tonight?

The heat in my face spirals downward and I have to resist the urge to cross my arms as my nipples harden and brush against the fabric of my dress.

As Dominick returns to his seat, the gentleman on the right takes his seat as well. A light smile touches his lips, the dark planes of his face highlighted in the golden light of the candles. The angular nose and square jaw give him a sharp appearance, harsh even but not unappealing.

Only a touch of gray at the temples hint that his age approaches anything past twenty-five. His body is honed to near perfection, the muscles clearly defined beneath the black knit shirt and well-fitting black dress pants.

It's then I realize everyone surrounding me is dressed in black. Even Dylan and Jacob. I'm in white. Innocence. Untouched.

I doubt it's a coincidence and I suddenly feel like the virgin about to be sacrificed.

"Gabrielle."

Dominick's voice interrupts my thoughts. He inclines his head towards the man and woman seated on each side of me.

"May I introduce our dinner companions, Vivienne and Kenneth." His voice fills the room, rich, refined, much like the house and the furnishings.

I nod silently at Kenneth but it is Vivienne that captures my attention, startled by her porcelain beauty. Wide-as-saucer eyes look at me unblinking, the dark half-moon of lashes above and below sharply contrasted by the alabaster skin. But there's no innocence reflected in the cool blue depths.

My attention is drawn back to Dominic. The intensity of his gaze holds my own.

"Tonight you will refer to Kenneth and myself as Sir. Vivienne you may address as Lady V or Ma'am."

His directive takes a moment to register. As if setting a match to a firecracker, the rebel in my soul sizzles at the instruction to use the titles of Sir or Ma'am.

If you can't speak to me with respect, Gabrielle, maybe you should go live elsewhere.

The memory of my aunt still makes me nauseous at times.

Surely, he can't be serious? I lean back in the chair, cross my legs and steeple my fingers beneath my chin. I start to smile at the joke, but the unchanging expressions of either my host or my dinner companions clue me in that no humor was intended.

This will challenge you, maybe even touch some parts of yourself you thought long buried or forgotten.

Lily's words quell any uncertainty faster than I would have thought possible a day earlier. Hell, an hour earlier I would have laughed at someone giving me the same orders. But I didn't want to disappoint her.

I nod my head, unwilling to trust my voice or my rebellious nature.

"You will speak your answer, Gabrielle. So we know there is no misunderstanding."

His voice, calm but forceful, never rises a note. His eyes never leave mine, the gaze a more intimate caress than many I'd experienced. He knew more than I wanted him to know. The compulsion to look away, just to prove to myself and to him that I can, presses behind my temples.

Gazing down at my crossed legs, I wait a second then return my eyes to his. "Yes, sir."

"Excellent." Dominick smiles and for that second we are the only two people in the room. The others fade into the woodwork. There's a quality to his smile, a hint of promise and challenge written in the tiny lines that hug the corners of his mouth.

Awareness tingles a path down my spine, circling around the juncture of my legs where the velvet cushion cradles my flesh. Not just an awareness of him as a man, of his strength and dominance.

It is a new awareness of me as a woman, recognition for the first time of desires I had never dared give life for fear they would bring ostracism and ridicule.

I've kept these parts of me hidden for so long – the desires, the wants, the need – afraid I could not have them. And now they were being delivered to me in limousines by messengers from my dreams.

Dinner is quite delightful, served almost invisibly by the woman I'd met at the door. Her role in the evening intrigues me the most. She hasn't spoken, nor has anyone spoken to her, yet they communicate with little more than a look or gesture.

The food slides over my pallet, teases the senses – caviar, oysters, veal ossobuco, fresh asparagus, Indian rice, sweet melon with pomegranate and kiwi – a treat after the mystery cuisine served in the campus cafeteria.

Wine is poured with the first course - a half glass only - and when that is gone we are served water. I finally relax around the third course and join in the conversation, finding Kenneth and Dominick intelligent and witty.

Kenneth enjoys playing the devil's advocate on virtually every issue, a role I normally assume in class or with my few friends. There is nothing better, in my opinion, than a good debate.

Dominick's opinions are strong on any subject and while he's polite about listening to what I have to say he disagrees with just about every position I take. I can tell by the corner glances to Kenneth or Lady V he's testing my patience or resolve. He wants to push my buttons.

I've had years of practice at keeping my feelings to myself. He'll need to come at me with more than reverse psychology.

I refrain from addressing either gentleman during the meal, either by name or title. Neither complain and I let Dominick's directive slip from my memory.

Vivienne remains mostly silent, responding only when either gentleman addresses her directly. I try several times to draw her into the conversation, but Kenneth speaks on her behalf, a characteristic I find both annoying and challenging.

Are the women in their world all silent unless the men require their participation? That doesn't sit well with me. It doesn't take a rocket scientist to know why. I'd been a guest as a kid in what should have been my home. Jon and Lily will be sorely disappointed if that's what they expect of me.

DESCENT
CHAPTER FIVE

Her demeanor piques my curiosity, as does her beauty and I think back to the rules I'd been given on the ride over.

"I have a question," I venture at the end of the meal, folding my napkin and placing it besides my plate.

"I would be surprised if you didn't have several," Kenneth jokes, shifting in his chair and leaning his elbows on the table. "What would you like to ask us, Gabrielle?"

"I'm curious about the women here tonight." I twirl the stem of my empty wine glass between my fingers. "Viv... Lady V," I concede, not wanting to lose the war over a skirmish, "And the woman who has served this delicious meal, are they not allowed to speak or answer for themselves?"

Dominick cocks his head slightly to the left, his eyes roaming over Lady V with a possessive glare. Her own gaze meets his briefly, then looks down, a hint of pink blossoming high on the sharp slash of her cheekbones.

Without taking his eyes off of her, Dominick answers my question with a question. "When you go to work, are you the same person as when you are with friends? Do you talk and act the same way?"

I shake my head, the sway of my hair skimming over the bare skin at my back. "Of course not. Work is work. Home is home."

"For Vivienne, tonight is like being at work. She has agreed to be my submissive tonight and so she follows certain rules we have agreed upon."

"She agrees to be ignored and have someone speak for her? Why would anyone do that?" The shock must be evident in my voice, and I'm certain on my face as well. The rules equate to being treated like a child. I'd had enough of that with my aunt and uncle to know.

Now his eyes slide to me. "Why did you?"

I blink rapidly and my mouth opens and closes like a fish stranded on dry land. "I didn't agree to any such rules."

"Not those, no," Dominick inclines his head toward Vivienne. "But she did. And you agreed to other rules. Did you not agree to call me and Kenneth Sir and address Vivienne as Lady V? Those are your rules for tonight, Gabrielle. There will be others; but I assure you nothing you do not agree to."

I take a sip of water to give myself time to calm down.

Rule #1: You're in charge.

The idea appeals to me.

"Then she's really the one in charge," I say out loud before I think about it, inclining my head toward Vivienne.

Dominick laughs at this, his broad body shaking with the amusement he finds in my words. "In a way, yes. She has agreed to follow my rules but how I enforce them is strictly up to me. She gives me the power and trusts that I will not abuse it."

Trust. There's that word again. With trust comes power. But who has the power?

"That's a lot of trust."

"It most certainly is," he agrees, and lifts his hand, palm extended outward to Vivienne.

She rises immediately and goes to Dominick's side. She stands where he indicates, to his left but to the back of his chair, her smile seemingly genuine. She places a possessive hand on his shoulder and he lifts it to kiss her fingers.

"And it is a trust I take extremely seriously. Viv and I have known each other a long time, so we have that level of confidence with each other."

The other woman appears from nowhere and I wonder what rules she has chosen to obey.

Kenneth answers my unasked question. "She is my pet tonight."

I bristle at the word. "Pet?"

"It is a term of endearment. Bottom. Sub. Slave." He studies her, his face wistful. "Pet."

The second woman mirrors Vivienne's actions, moving to Kenneth's side. But she kneels, resting her cheek against his thigh. He strokes her hair gently, almost reverently.

"These are words which hold different meanings. Kylia has agreed to no limits tonight. She is mine in every sense of the word."

I play with the edge of my napkin, and shift in my chair but my eyes are all for Kylia and Kenneth. "And if you told her to put her hand to the flame of the candle, would she do it?"

"Without hesitation," Kenneth beams proudly. He stops stroking Kylia's hair and she rises to her feet but stays by his side.

Would he prove the very point to me? My heart races. I

lean forward in my chair, prepare to snatch the candle from the table if Kenneth so much as twitches a muscle.

He lifts a hand, palm outward, in silent assurance. "But I would never do such a thing. Just as there are rules for her and Viv, there are expectations for Dominick and myself. We would never break the faith of those who give us their submission. Think of it as a parent with a child."

Not a great analogy for me, and something in my face must give away my distaste.

"Of a good, loving parent with a child," he amends. "Their trust in us is a gift. One which, as Dominick pointed out, a true dominant would never abuse."

We're back to the power aspect.

I can't help but let my thoughts wander to my aunt and uncle. I would never have trusted them with such openness. Then again, they'd never done anything to deserve it.

Is this what Lily and Jon wanted me to learn? They are willing to earn my trust. To believe they would not abuse the trust they asked of me?

I look at Vivienne and Kylia. They certainly didn't seem abused. I'd never seen anyone look so content.

"There's one more rule for you, Gabrielle."

I look to Dominick and the corner of his mouth has hitched up. It almost quivers with whatever he's holding back. This ought to be good.

"You are not allowed to reach orgasm without permission."

It's my turn with the half smile. I don't really mind this rule. It's not like I planned on masturbating on the table for the fearsome foursome tonight. Even if I did, I think my nerves would keep me from reaching any kind of happy ending.

My night with Jon and Lily had been...unusual. While

tonight certainly fit the category of unusual, I think it went a bit beyond.

But I'd had to ask permission for everything as a child living in a home that wasn't my home. May I have a glass of milk? May I get up from the table? May I go to my room for bed?

Too often the answer had been no. Even more often the yes came with strings attached. Yes, if you clean the kitchen first. Yes, if you bring in the mail.

I bump up against the unpleasant memory, the edges sharp, jagged. But this is not about my aunt and uncle, I remind myself.

I nod my head.

"However, because it is your first lesson, you are most likely to receive permission if you ask for it tonight."

"Most likely?" I've learned it's the clarifying words you have to watch out for.

Kenneth inclines his head toward me, answering instead, "We wouldn't want to make any promises. It's a dominant's prerogative to take the sub where she or he needs to go. Not where they want to go."

"And it's not just for tonight's encounter." Dominick's added caveat speeds up my heart. I can almost guess what's coming (or not). "But for the entire weekend."

This just got interesting.

BOTTOM
CHAPTER SIX

"You are not allowed to orgasm without express permission from Lily, Jon, or your dominant for the evening until Lily releases you from your submission. Do you understand?"

I think of my ride here with Jacob and how quickly he revved my engine. While I'd not taken him up on the offer, I certainly had plans to use his memory later in fantasy land. But I nod again. In for a penny...a frustrated penny apparently.

"Please speak your agreement with this rule, Gabrielle. There are consequences if you disobey."

Consequences. Already I'm thinking there's no way anyone would know if I got home and masturbated to Jacob's memory or the oh-so-hot memory of me and Lily and Jon. What does it matter if I agree?

"I understand." I lift my water glass in salute, the clear liquid sloshing with the tremble of my hand. "No orgasms without permission." Then as a reluctant addition, I murmur, "Yes, sir."

Dominick nods but he's looking at me from beneath his

lashes, like he's reading the wayward path of my dirty thoughts. I maintain the heavy eye contact. I can play chicken as well as the next person.

Kenneth clears his throat and pushes from his chair. I cut my eyes to him. He's shaking his head but the grin on his face suggests he's stepping from the line of fire more than laughing over the new rule.

The dinner dishes are cleared while we continue to talk, the conversation steering toward softer topics of my studies and plans after graduation.

As if on some hidden cue, both Vivienne and Kylia move behind Dominick, each with a hand on his broad shoulders. He relaxes into their touch, arms folded, every ounce of intensity in his gaze focused on me.

Kenneth's dark eyes assess me in great detail but he's not moving yet.

I raise one eyebrow at Dominick, wanting to return the challenge in his perusal.

"Time for dessert, Gabrielle."

The deep voice ripples across the table. Goosebumps skitter up my arm and adrenaline shoots into my veins.

I swirl my water glass and study him over the edge of the crystal. "Really? What's for dessert?"

"You."

I say nothing taking another sip of water to unstick my tongue from the roof of my mouth. Then Kenneth rises from the table and moves behind my chair. I freeze, certain I've heard him wrong.

Afraid I haven't.

Hoping I didn't.

This is at the heart of what Lily wants me to learn. Trust. Trust in her and Jon. Trust in myself. Nothing real inside of me is telling me I'm in danger.

That's not exactly true.

Every fiber of my being tells me I'm about to be challenged in every way conceivable. So far tonight, they've pushed all my buttons. The use of words like sir and ma'am for simple conversation. Asking permission with only the promise of possibility it will be granted.

It's like they reached into my past and pulled out the major wounds and placed a salt shaker next to the gaping holes.

But it's not fear sounding an alarm.

It's anticipation coursing through my body.

Dominick's gaze never wavers. Kenneth rests a hand on my elbow, exerting a gentle pressure. I uncross my legs and stand.

Kenneth leans down and speaks in my ear. "Do you remember your safe word?"

I nod.

"Say it."

The abrupt command startles me and I have to swallow twice to find my voice. "Lily."

My heart stops. The breath sticks in my throat.

Behind Dominick and the two women Lily and Jon emerge from the hallway, their arms entwined around one another. I release the air held captive in my lungs, the tension flows out of me on the rush.

Tears burn at the corner of my eyes and I blink them away, embarrassed by the show of emotion. A half-sob, half-laugh escapes.

Jon winks at me. Lily smiles and blows me a kiss.

My thoughts at seeing them are jumbled but clear at the same time. I want to fall into their arms, insinuate myself between them and let them wrap me in that same cocoon of warmth I woke to the morning after our first night together.

I don't understand the surety that relaxes my posture or lightens the weight in my chest. I just know it's there.

The two of them disappear and a loneliness falls around me. I breathe deeply. I'm used to being alone so the spark of want that flashes at Jon and Lily's presence is unfamiliar and uncomfortable. But they are here, and I trust as much as I can that they will be back.

"Now we begin," Dominick announces.

Vivienne pulls out the chair as Dominick pushes to his feet.

The three of them move in unison. Kenneth urges me forward and I let him propel me from the table. I see the room in a haze, the edges blurry and unclear. The center of my view – Dominick – is focused and sharp however.

I watch his legs as they stretch with each step, the way the dark fabric of his trousers tighten around his thighs. His shoulders look wider but perhaps it is only because the two women flanking him are so small.

The procession halts in front of a door. Dominick closes the distance between us. The nearness presses at the edges of my claustrophobia and for a moment I am a stranger in my own skin. Our breaths mingle. Heat pulses between us. The heady aroma of his cologne circles me and I have to fight the urge to look away, trying to find myself in the tight embrace where he readily looms.

His hands lift to my throat, my breath pausing, my heart suspended as his fingers lift the chain around my neck. He withdraws the three keys nestled between my breasts.

"All of your lessons will deal with trust, Gabrielle." The voice shimmies its way along my skin, the tidal wave of gooseflesh crashing against my neck. My nipples harden instantly. My knees give a wobble.

"But it is mostly about learning to trust yourself. For now, though, will you trust me?"

I consider the question carefully. I do not know these people and in any other situation my answer would have come without hesitation: no. This is not a normal situation, however. Very little about the last week has been normal. I take a deep breath.

I know what I should say. What he – what all of them want me to say. "I will trust you because Lily and Jon trust you."

Do I believe it?

As much as I believe anything else at the moment. I wouldn't give him the passcode to my ATM card, but I'd walk with him to the ATM.

Dominick smiles. "Do you remember the limits Lily explained to you?"

I think back then it dawns on me. Our conversation in the library. "She said I would not be harmed in any way."

Dominick nods in agreement. "Do you understand what that means? The semantics between harm and hurt?"

I consider the words and more of Lily's explanation filters into my head. "Hurt, some pain to either my body or maybe my ego. Harm, a true injury."

"Correct. If at any time you wish to stop, simply use your safeword."

I nodded silently then add, "Yes, sir."

If I'm going to play the game, I have to play to win.

This time Dominick beams at me and the smile would be dazzling if I didn't have the memory of Jon's slow grin or the sensuous quirk of Lily's lips.

I wish again they were here with me. Then I remember

they are, hidden perhaps, but still here. I feel them as strange as it is to admit that. The knowledge comforts me more than I would have thought possible.

"Then will you give me one of your keys and let the lesson begin?" Dominick extends his hand.

He won't take it from me. That would defeat the lesson I realize. I have to be the one to choose. I have to be the one to open the door and step into the classroom.

Yes, I want Lily and Jon here but neither Kenneth, Lady V, nor Dominick are hard on the eyes. Not to mention Jacob and Dylan. And Kylia...she intrigues me in other ways. She may be silent but the woman's eyes...as cliche' as it sounds, what I see behind those eyes sends heat ziplining to my girly bits.

Then Jacob and Dylan are waiting in the wings as well.

I'm not sure I fit into the sultry line up of Jon and Lily's friends. Then again, have I ever really fit anywhere?

I pull one key from the chain and resettle the remaining keys gently between my breasts. Dominick's eyes linger and where his gaze rests, my flesh burns.

The metal key is cool in my fingers, and I study the engraving on the shaft of the key. What mysterious message does it hold?

Deep breath.

Now or never, Bree. What'll it be?

BARED
CHAPTER SEVEN

I hand Dominick the key. He opens the door and disappears down a staircase.

The two women follow. Kenneth stands a few feet away, his stance casual, arms crossed over the defined swell of his chest. He watches, perhaps waiting for me to flee.

I hold the door open, noticing for the first time the rapid rise and fall of my chest, the erratic drum of my pulse and the incredible throbbing between my legs.

I can still make an escape, I reason, circling the gold doorknob with my middle finger. Lily and Jon are near. I can go back to school and pretend this never happened.

The weight of that last thought is heavy on my shoulders. I fill my lungs with a deep breath and let it exhale in a burst, releasing the tension in my limbs at the same time.

I can go back to being exactly who I was before last Saturday night.

Boring.

Unsatisfied.

Incomplete.

My exploration of this darker, undiscovered side of

myself feels natural if uncomfortable. I am meant for this, meant for the pleasures Jon and Lily have introduced to me. There is fear, but not doubt.

The first step requires a voluntary effort on the part of my muscles to listen to the signals my brain send out. Each step becomes easier.

A thin veil of light beckons from below and I narrow my attention on that. The stairs spill into a large room that can only be described as dungeonesque.

Red brick walls. Bare cement floors. Massive beams overhead run the length of the cavernous room. The room is in shadow, lit only by flickering candles. Hundreds of them dot the walls and floor. The light comes from everywhere but isn't strong enough to reach the far walls of the room. A faint undertone tickles my nose and wraps around my shoulders, warm, inviting, dangerous.

The smell of sex.

Kenneth walks from behind me to stand with the others. The fab four stand together, poised center stage for all practical purposes. I am both the audience and the main attraction.

The backdrop to the unfolding drama catches my eye: a large four poster bed. A dark frame surrounds the mattress; it looks to be larger than a king if that's possible. A crisp, white sheet covers the mattress along with a jumble of pillows at the headboard.

A shiver curls through my body before I can tamp it down.

"Are you afraid?" The voice echoes against the brick, fading into the shadows hugging the corners of the room.

I tilt my head to the left and right, testing my options. I am afraid but my body hums with the excitement of the fear, each nuance of my flesh alive to me like never before.

But the fear is still there and it begins to chase around the other thoughts inside my head. Pushing them forward. Prodding them from the dark nether regions of my mind and into my consciousness. Thoughts I'd never allowed myself to explore now collide with reality.

I look past the fab four into the shadows beyond them, wondering if two pairs of eyes are looking back at me. Lily and Jon are close. They said they would be. I can feel them with me.

"Yes," I finally answer. "But only that I'll fail those that have put their trust in me."

Dominic smiles. Kenneth nods. The women remain silent, expressionless except for their eyes. Their eyes say anticipation.

"Come to me, Gabrielle."

The hypnotic pull of Dominic's voice pushes away my random thoughts and draws me forward. Each step raps sharply in the quiet of the room. He traps my gaze, his eyes never leaving mine. I wait for some sign of hesitation on his part, some mirror of the uncertainty coursing through my veins. The heat of the rushing blood fills my cheeks and cascades down my neck, pooling between my legs. My nipples harden and the brush of the material against the twin peaks reminds me of Jon's hands on my body. Lily's lips on my breasts.

As I draw near, Dominic extends his hand, palm up, long fingers bent slightly. The curvature of his hand reminds me of a cup waiting to be filled. I slip my hand into his, another shiver chasing the heat down my spine when he closes his fingers gently around mine.

He leads me deeper into the room. I watch the play of muscles in his back and shoulders as they tighten and flex with his movements. His upper arms are as big as my thighs. Well-defined legs taper from a firm backside and I can't help but wonder what he looks like nude. The surprising thought ignites the heat in my cheeks.

Physically, Dominick can do me great harm and probably never break a sweat. But I don't fear him. Well...ok...maybe I do a little. I look again into the darkness.

Please be there.

Kenneth and the two women fan out behind us but don't come closer. We stop at the foot of the bed. There's another table on the far side, its contents covered from view by a towel but even covered I could tell what it was. Interesting.

"Undress for me, Gabrielle."

Dominick's voice fills the vast basement. The implication of his words skitters across my brain. I tense, instinct pressing me back but the sinewy granite of Kenneth's torso molds with the bare curve of my spine, halting my retreat and setting off an explosion of sensations within my body.

I close my eyes and breathe in slowly, the air filling my lungs. I can trace the rush of blood through my body.

I'd never been entirely comfortable with my body, much less with being nude in front of strangers. My night with Jon and Lily pushed the limits of everything I ever imagined experiencing sexually.

I find the new freedom to be invigorating.

I reach over my head and release the clasp holding together the dress, then let the dress slip from my shoulders. Four pairs of eyes are riveted to my body – the weight a physical caress.

I step out of the dress and hand it to Kylia, who's moved next to me as silently as she had been all night. The cold air teases the warmth of embarrassment surrounding my face as I wait in the eternity of their silence.

Then absent any signal I could decipher, the four of them move toward me, a cage of sensuous flesh closing in. Their presence overwhelms my sense of fight or flight and all I can do is stand and breathe as they near.

Kenneth and Dominick flank me in the front, a solid wall of muscle and determination. But the arousal so evident in their faces is what keeps my eyes on them, mirror images of lust and eagerness.

Lips slightly parted. The steady rise and fall of their chests. The thrum of a pulse visible in the strong line of their throats.

I'd not experienced such raw desire in my life, especially not directed at me. It's quite intimidating but again, my fight or flight response is stilled in the atmosphere.

Vivienne and Kylia each take ahold of an arm and lead me to the covered table. A doctor's exam table, with the head slightly elevated while the bottom vees outward with two stirrups.

I am positioned on the table. They draw my hands above my head, press a palm to the inside of my knee to open my legs spread slightly. The leather is firm yet gentle, restrictive but not unyielding. It creaks in the silence of the room and I swear I can hear my heartbeat echo against the walls. My pulse quickens. The position mirrors my memories of Jon and Lily, vulnerable, open.

Vivienne places my feet in the stirrups, her hands gliding over my calves and thighs as she adjusts the table. When her hand dips between my legs, I rear up and close my legs.

Dominick shakes his head and approaches the side of the table. "That is an instinct I would resist, sweet Gabrielle."

Kenneth moves to stand at the end of the table. He

brandishes a straight razor, the dim light reflecting off the silver blade.

Kenneth's eyes challenge mine as he places the razor on the table then opens his hands wide to show me they are empty. My breathing gets a little rapid and heat moves through my body. I tense although he has not moved an inch towards me. I want to ask what will happen. I want to, but I don't. I want to trust in Lily and Jon but the doubt still tickles at the back of my brain.

He sits and slowly wraps his fingers gently around my ankles, and I suck in a sharp breath at first contact of his flesh with mine. Those strong hands hold me gently but without leeway. My pulse quickens with the anticipation.

Without losing eye contact, he slides his hands up the outer curve of my calves then snakes inward to press softly but insistently on the inside of my knees where my legs clench together tightly. I relax and let him open me, baring me completely for his gaze, yet his eyes never leave mine.

His hands linger, a tangible weight on my body with the mere whisper of a touch. My skin tingles to life where his hands own me. The gooseflesh skitters to life to meet the graze that stilled me with such a simple gesture. Desire and hesitation spark like a flare inside me.

I look to his eyes but Jon fills my vision. The intimacy of those hands remind me of Lily's possessive and knowing caress and the hesitation slips away. Their presence fills my heart. I hear them inside my head. They're doing this because I need it. Because I want them. It's not only the surrender that appeals to me, I realize; it's the trust that it implies.

Kylia moved to Kenneth's side and I hear the clatter and clank of items moving around the covered tray. I lift up slightly on my elbows to see what they are doing but

Kenneth slaps the inside of my thigh, a sharp sting like lightning to my core.

I jump and yelp, surprised by the contact and the involuntary contraction of my pussy muscles. A deep, almost painful pulse throbs in my clit.

"Dominick, perhaps you and Vivienne can keep our guest busy so she's not tempted to peek." A delicious smile spreads across Kenneth's dark face and he observes beneath hooded eyes as Dominick and Vivienne approach from each side.

TOUCH
CHAPTER EIGHT

My nipples harden and I arch back into the table as their hands move closer. I cannot evade the first touch, a gentle touch really, on the curve of my hip and the swell of my right breast.

White hot shards of pleasure zip through me as they trail their hands upward along the side of my body, caressing, teasing, pinching. Vivienne's nails scorch a path across my stomach. I am trapped and I moan with the agony and ecstasy of it.

Oh the sweet agony of those fingers!

That is when I notice Kenneth and Kylia between my legs. She rubs a cool, creamy lotion over the flesh. Shaving cream by the sudsy feel of it. A hint of menthol reaches my nose.

I close my eyes against the rhythmic pounding in my pussy. The sensation of all their hands on me at once is too much to bear. My lips part and a breath escapes with a ragged moan.

Dominick's voice parts the haze of my ecstasy. "Remember, you are not allowed to come, Gabrielle."

My eyes open and he is all that fills my vision. I am lost for words though my body is singing the Halleluia chorus. "Wh-what?"

Vivienne's attention moves over my palm at this instant, tracing a circle in the center, then moves up my arm to the arc of my neck. There is a brief pause at the hollow beneath my ear – it's a spot that drives me wild – and I cannot help but moan again.

Dominick's hand skims beneath my chin and lifts until my eyes flutter to his, while the other hand moves quickly to my nipple. He pinches it sharply. I gasp at the sensation riding close to the pain/pleasure border.

"First, you have not asked for permission." His words are succinct, enunciated, precise. "Second, the answer is no."

"But you said –"

"We are sadists, sweetness."

As if to prove his point, Vivienne sucks my nipple into her mouth, grazing it hard with her teeth. A memory of Lily stirs and an electric current zips right to my pussy and I groan.

"Besides, I'm not ready for this to be over."

I groan again.

He tsks slowly at me. "You will regret disobedience."

How I'm supposed to avoid orgasm is not something that seems possible but I concentrate as Kenneth and Kylia begin to shave the hair from my pussy. It is a feeling that is odd and disconcerting as they pull the flesh taut then scrape the blade along the skin, ever so careful with each flick of the wrist.

Dominick eyes me closely, his fingers still pinching the hardened peak of my breast, a dark and twisty smile diving into the dimples that hollow in his sharply chiseled cheekbones.

He smells of aftershave and leather, a heady combination that swirls in the dimly lit room to mix with the aroma of my own arousal. I am so close to the edge I fear I will not be able to hold off much longer.

"I can't take much more." The tortured whisper rasps out. My resistance - and the lie - trembles on my lips.

"But you will." His breath rushes against my cheek. "Because I wish it. Because Lily and Jon wish it."

Lily and Jon.

Their memory only serves to heighten the peak of my arousal, an invisible caress that finds places more intimate than my body. I fight because that is all I know.

Fight against the want.

Fight against the desire.

Fight against myself.

I've been fighting so long against the things inside me I'm not sure I can live any other way.

But Jon and Lily...they are showing me I do not have to fight, or at least not fight alone. There are others. Others who know what I want and will give it to me, freely and without judgment. Can I take what they offer?

Can I ask for it?

Before my mind can settle on an answer I realize that Kenneth is rubbing a cool gel on my newly bared skin. The others have backed away. Vivienne is curled against Dominick's side, his arm possessively draped around her shoulder.

The evidence of his erection beneath the black trousers or the flush on Vivienne's face are unmistable. Behind them, I see the large four-poster bed and wonder what's next? A delicious warmth settles between my legs, a sharp contrast to the cool lotion Kenneth had used moments earlier.

Kenneth extends a hand to me as he rises. I am afraid but my body hums with the excitement of the fear, each nuance of my flesh alive.

But the fear is still there and it begins to chase around the other thoughts inside my head. Pushing them forward. Prodding them from the dark nether regions of my mind and into my consciousness. Thoughts I'd never allowed myself to explore now collide with reality.

Fear makes you see things differently.

Can I let go enough to learn what Lily and Jon want me to learn? Trust is earned, but it's also given. Am I willing to give this to Lily and Jon?

Kenneth and Dominick are at my side now, and without a word Kenneth sweeps me into his arms. Where he touches me, my skin hums. I'm naked and vulnerable, my entire side pressed against a man I'd never met until a few hours ago.

My hands press against his chest, to steady myself though I don't feel the least bit of a burden in his arms. His hold on me, like the dark gaze he levels at me, are solid as the proverbial rock.

But I press my palms against the massive plane of his torso also because I want to feel the rhythm of his heart beneath my hands. It's there. My brain unconsciously fills in words to go with the sensations.

Steady. *Jon*.

Vibrant. *Lily*.

After he places me on the mattress, I am bound to the frame, my hands above my head, my legs spread slightly, soft cuffs holding me with the strength of their binds but soft as a lover. The panic from the shower earlier with Jon weasels its way forward.

"Put your hands together, Bree," Dominick instructs but I hesitate. My heart is a pounding force in my chest and Lily's name hovers on my tongue.

"Feel this?" He maneuvers my hand to some mechanism I cannot see. "Pull here and the cuffs release. Try it."

I slide a finger into the metal ring, tug softly and a *click* releases the cuff.

Lily and Jon remembered. They knew...and they remembered.

My heart steadies into a slower rhythm as Vivienne connects the cuffs once more.

Warm air caresses the newly bared skin at the juncture of my thighs, a warmth that spreads slowly like honey across my body. The leather is firm yet gentle, restrictive but not unyielding...much like the hands of my lovers. I imagine it is their hands holding me. Jon's hands at my ankles, holding me open. Lily's hands on my wrists, holding me up.

When I look up again, Dominick, Kenneth, and Lady V are wearing leather masks, their features hidden, blending into the darkness around them.

Kylia hovers at my side, her soft features impassive but not hardened. Her flawless skin and deep set eyes appear lit from within and I study the expression for a moment before she shows me a silk blindfold. She slips it across my eyes.

In that last blink of vision, I see the corner of her mouth lift into an interesting smirk. I'd call it anticipatory or predatory; I just couldn't decide which took the lead at the moment.

The blindfold is not solid – its gauzy nature permits me some semblance of sight. The world around me is bathed in film noir enhanced beneath the hazy filter of silk. I hear a door open and snap my head in that direction. Bodies begin to move. Someone steps closer to the bed where I am bound, his weighty gaze a presence on my body.

The face is obscured by the mask and the gauzy film of silk. Dark clothing in a dark room blur the edges of shape and form.

I know instantly...even instinctively who it is though logic tells me Dominick is the one standing over me. He is the one in the room. I saw him put on the mask. But it's someone else before me now.

I can tell by the presence, the sharp intake of breath, the feel of his desire energizes the air. Or is it just wishful thinking on my part?

He's wearing black from head to toe, blending into the darkness of the room, a shadow, a silhouette. Hidden from me.

Except for the hands.

I see those strong hands and know they will be my undoing.

He's not moved since stepping into my line of sight but he's watching me. I know where the gaze touches my skin when it moves over my nude body and I want to either pull away from it or lean into it more. The duality of sensation floods my senses. How can I want something so much but be afraid of it as well?

There may be other people in the room but only one person is staring at me right now, perfuming the air with a lust to match my own.

My breathing gets a little rapid and heat moves through my body. I tense although he has not moved an inch toward me. I want to ask what will happen. I want to, but I won't. I already know. He moves toward me and I pull on the restraints.

The leather creaks in the silence of the room and I can hear my heartbeat echo against the walls. My pulse quickens and when he reaches out, I suck in a breath sharp with the anticipation at the first contact of his flesh with mine.

His touch hovers, moving over my body with whispered intent. I feel the heat of his skin if not his actual hand. My flesh tingles to life wherever his hands move. The goose-flesh rises to meet the caress that never comes. I look to his eyes and see deep into the soul looking back.

I feel his thoughts. Hear them inside my head. I know he does this because I need it. Because I need to learn this lesson of trust.

My nipples harden and I arch away as the hands move closer, a separate entity from the man standing there. It is like the desire burning inside – I don't consider it a part of me, have not accepted that I want this as much as I do. How can I? To admit it is to give it power. The power to hurt when it is taken away.

I cannot evade the first touch, a gentle caress really, on the curve of my hip. Oh, those fingers, the burn radiates from one point of contact. White hot shards of pleasure zip through me.

He draws the hand upward along the side of my body, cupping the swell of my breast, tracing the underside of my arm. I pull away with each inch of my flesh he claims, but I am trapped and I moan with the agony and ecstasy of the claustrophobic warmth.

The irony of my position is not lost of me. I'm bound but free. I pull away to arch into each touch. Giving myself so I can be taken.

His fingers move over my palm, tracing a circle in the

center, then move up my arm again, along the arch of my neck. There is a brief pause at the hollow beneath my ear - the spot that drives me wild - before it continues to my lips. My lips part, and the breath that escapes is ragged and tremulous.

"More?"

He's reminding me the power is mine. Reminding me I am in control. No one here will take what I do not give.

"Yes, sir."

I'm not sure if I'm more surprised by the answer, or that it took so long for me to say it.

Was this woman always hidden inside? How had I let her stay quiet all these years? Perhaps because hiding was easier than dealing with the consequences of revelation. I don't know how I managed to keep it all contained but I know I won't be able to do it again.

The ache of loss pierces my heart. The loss of this want, this freedom, of those who set it free.

Another touch shatters my thoughts and I writhe beneath the ministering. It's too much to bear. It steals away the protection of my control, carefully constructed over years, and brings me to the edge of vulnerability then cradles me and guides me back.

Once again the torturous journey begins, my nipple hardening as the destination crystalizes in heated clarity.

I gasp. He stops.

The heat of desire warms my skin.

"Do you wish me to continue?" He grazes my nipple with the tip of one finger, the touch only the briefest of contacts.

At my hesitation, he adds in a whisper against my ear, "It's ok to say yes to what you want. It's ok to say no."

The sensation is like lightening through me and the plea escapes. "Yes...please. Sir."

A laugh. It is a deep rumble that tells me he takes pleasure in making me beg. As a reward or punishment, I can't be sure which, he traces the outer edge of the areola, watching as the skin puckers. The ache intensifies...travels...then stops, the core of the burn buried deep within. There is an emptiness I know only he can fill.

"Do you want me?"

"Yes, sir." The word is breathless, barely audible to my ears but a smile lights the only thing visible to me behind the mask: the eyes. He laughs again.

"Good."

RESISTANCE
CHAPTER NINE

He starts to move his finger along my sides again, over the curve of my hip and down my thigh. I want to bend my legs but the restraints prevent all but the slightest movement. He caresses the underside of my knee and I jerk against the leather.

He releases my hands from the cuffs, tracing the tip of his finger down my arm to the crook of my elbow then to my underarm, finally to my breast.

"Touch yourself."

My body is on fire and there's nothing more that I want than to reach between my legs, plunge my fingers into my channel and drive away the need. Is giving in to this pleasure/pain a weakness? A flaw? Should I resist as I have always done?

People are watching. I think of the night Lily and Jon discovered me. The embarrassment. The desire.

"I can't—"

"You can." His face is instantly near mine and his breath rushes against my cheek.

He grazes the instep of my foot and my entire body

arches against the table. Leather stretches in protest and the air is filled with the sound of my breath being sucked inward, filling my lungs in quick, anguished seconds.

He pauses, letting me grow comfortable, letting me realize he'll stop when needed, push me when needed. My entire being is focused on this one point of contact, mere millimeters in diameter. In many ways I am like this touch, only a fraction of the whole waiting to be discovered, uncovered by him.

He moves again and my body trembles. I ask him, beg him, really. "Please...no more."

"But we are only just beginning."

His boots echo against the hard floor, moving away from me and into the blanket of darkness that envelops us. An eternal silence drifts on the waves of my heartbeat until he returns, his hands now hidden from my view. I meet his eyes, asking, searching, remembering the trust I have given.

He leans over my face, the taste of his lips and tongue fill my mouth and possess my soul. His leather-clad cheek caresses mine with infinite gentleness. The rush of his own breath fills my ears and echoes in the hollow parts of my soul.

There's a brush of his fingers against my lips, down my throat, trailing slowly down my torso. My body races ahead to the eventual destination and begins the burn before he arrives.

He cups the newly bared skin, still sensitive and cool at the juncture between my thighs, dancing along this line of flesh and nerves. He touches me everywhere but where I need it most. I push his hand to the juncture of my thighs but his resistance is better than my own.

"Touch yourself, Bree. Show me what you want."

I don't know what I want. I want him to touch me. To lead me, to take me where I need to go.

The fingers tease my clit, the entrance to my body.

Damn him. I can't ask for this. Too much in me rebels at the thought of asking for anything I want, at giving anyone that much control.

I fight because that is all I know. Fight against the want. Fight against the desire. Fight against myself.

The first real sense of fear teases the back of my mind. He knows my weaknesses. How will I resist?

I won't.

I can't.

I don't have to.

Because I am in control. Regardless of his answer, I am still in control.

Yes. Yes. Yes.

But I can't give the words life. I open my mouth, trying to force them out but my brain and my heart battle for control. I feel safe with the words in my head. I'm his. I'm hers. But giving them the to the world, even the small world in this room...the fear echoes in my heart.

"Give in to it, my sweet," his voice commands. "It's what I want. It's what you want. Tell me you're mine."

I want. I need.

But even standing at the edge I cannot put voice to the words. He has mercy, though, finding my fingers, driving me to the edge, driving me with my own need and desire.

"Remember, you are not allowed to come, Gabrielle," Dominick's voice rings out from the dark. "Not unless you ask permission."

Any further words or thoughts are stolen by the pressure of his hands on the inside of my channel, finding that sweet spot of pain and pleasure.

My nipples pucker and my chest heaves, drawing in air. The tension hums along my nerves and the gooseflesh skates across my flesh. I'm going to –

"Please, may I come?"

My salvation is uttered in a single word. "Yes."

I arch off the bed as the orgasm tackles me like a force of nature. Muscles tighten all over my body to try and control the sweet assault but it is as useless as controlling the tides or the whispy path of clouds. It won't be contained.

My breath, arrested in my lungs, will not escape. Lights dance in the corners of my eyes until a voice, insisting in a soft caress of breath, tells me, "Breathe, Bree."

And like that air rushes in and out of my lungs, chasing back the lights, feeding the burn of the orgasm as it floods my body with endorphins and serotonin. The perfume of lust fills the air around me and carries me into the darkness.

INFRACTION
CHAPTER TEN

I awake in the limo on the way home but Jacob's voice murmurs for me to sleep and I don't have the strength to protest. I don't remember being carried to my room, nor do I remember being lain upon my bed. I simply remember feeling content.

When I wake the next time, I stretch lazily beneath the covers. I'm naked, a state I'm beginning to get comfortable with and enjoy. My muscles are a little sore from the night's activities but overall I'm none the worse for wear. In fact, I feel pretty damn good. At least until I look at the clock. I'd felt so good last night, I'd slept through the morning classes and now I'm late for work.

Oh well. My schedule is light today and I doubt anyone missed me in study group. I kick my legs free of the covers and slide from the bed. I catch sight of my reflection in the mirror. A rosy glow darkens the contours of my cheeks but other than a not-to-be-contained smile, I can see no evidence to indicate last night's adventures.

The chain swinging between the valley of my breasts is now shy one key. The fearsome foursome. Dominick said

I'm supposed to learn to trust myself. I'd stopped trusting others and by doing that, I guess I'd stopped trusting myself as well.

Is this a lesson I can learn?

That was the intent of Dickens' three ghosts, wasn't it? To teach Ebeneezer a lesson. What did I learn, then, from my encounter with Dominick?

Dominick had told me I must ask for something – an orgasm of all things - and that I was *almost* guaranteed, at least last night, to receive it. So, it was about trusting him to keep his word.

So why couldn't I touch myself? Did I not trust myself?

There were other moments, I realize now. When Jacob had asked permission to touch me in the car. When Lily and Jon appeared almost instantaneously at the use of my safe-word. Dominick's permission to reach orgasm. Or was that Jon?

At the time I was certain it was Jon's face behind the mask, Jon's hands on my body. It was dark. I was blind-folded. But this morning, the memory is fuzzy at the edges.

They were intent on proving themselves worthy of my trust.

Maybe earning my trust is as important to Lily and Jon as giving it is to me. If I've picked someone who would work so hard to gain my trust, doesn't that mean I've chosen well? I can trust my own judgment. That has to count for something.

I tuck away that mental note, refocusing on my efforts to get dressed. I grab the shower bucket and my towel and head down to the bathroom.

Dominick had given me a great gift last night (something other than the mind-blowing orgasm!) and I hope I have the chance to thank him.

In the shower the water is warm and tingly over my skin. I finger the two keys remaining, wondering what delights they will bring in the next forty-eight hours.

As I pass the sudsy shower puff between my legs, the newly denuded state of my pubis is strange to me. I run my fingers along the bared skin, remembering Kenneth's hands between my legs. Dominick's and Vivienne's hands and mouths everywhere else.

Damn. The scent of my arousal fills the shower stall and I listen for any sound that I'm not alone. I've got time for a quickie, I realize, replacing the soapy puff with my own fingers. It doesn't take me long to skirt along the edge of sweet release.

My mind plays over the scene from last night. Jacob's sultry smile. Lily's talented tongue. Jon's long body pressed up against mine. Dominick's voice coming at me in the darkness.

You're not allowed to come without permission, Gabrielle.

My fingers still and I start to argue with myself.

No one will know.

You'll know.

But I'm not going to tell.

That's not the point.

Then what is the point?

You want to trust Lily and Jon?

Yes.

Then you have to be someone worthy of trust in return.

Dammit to hell and back. I cross my arms and petulantly stamp my foot, the water splashing up from the tile floor.

This was going to be a long weekend.

I shower and change then head to work. But my mind is

anywhere but on the stack of books to be reshelved or the thousand questions on how to find this or that.

As I am leaving work a messenger arrives and delivers a single white rose with a note. The card simply says, "Midnight."

Heat swirls around my belly and my hands tremble. So do the folds of my sex. I flash back to the shower this morning and my frustrated state makes my knees shimmy in sudden weakness.

I laugh at myself. How can one word inspire such a reaction? Because I know ... or at least I can guess...what will happen after midnight.

Hopefully something to take care of my frustration.

As delicious as the weekend is so far, and as busy as my mind is thinking about tonight, I'm still a student and my studies would only be put off so much. I have a mid-term due in a few days so after work I head to the library. I'm having trouble concentrating on the textbook in front of me, however.

I'd found a quiet corner in the library. The place is mostly deserted on a Saturday morning. Who wants to be at the library on a Saturday?

The hard chair presses against my ass and I wiggle as if it will give any more but all that really does is grind my still sensitive flesh against the unyielding surface.

Who knew orgasms could be so draining?

I start to laugh and have to slap my hand over my mouth. It is the library and even though I'm relatively alone in this corner, noise travels in the cavernous building. And you're never really alone in here. I find people hiding in the nooks and crannies all the time when I'm working the stacks.

As if the universe wants to prove my point, footsteps *tap tap tap* behind me, the growing sound slow in the silence around me. Something I can only call familiarity tugs at me and I turn toward the sound and see Lily stalking forward.

The look on her face sends shivers chasing the heat coiling in my belly. Contrails of gooseflesh follow in its wake and my world narrows down to her. Her eyes. Her mouth. Her attention.

She's wearing a black leather jacket, silver studs and black straps criss-crossing the front and sides in a complicated pattern that keeps the eye guessing and moving. The jacket's zipper is pulled about halfway up and if there's anything beneath the jacket I'll dance naked in the cafeteria.

It's the pants that really draw the eye and keep it. She's dipped in the purple leather, her long legs divebombing into a pair of ankle boots. The pants hug and tease and promise with each stride. I'm wet already. I can feel my arousal dampen my panties and scent the air around me.

Lily closes the remaining distance, lowering her gaze as she approaches. She presses one finger to my shoulder and as I lean back against the chair, she straddles me, settling in my lap with a wiggle and a sultry purr.

A deep inhale tells me she can smell my arousal and she rolls her head back and around her shoulders like a contented feline. Her tongue darts out to taste the air and lick the bow of her top lip.

"Sweet." The words rolls off her tongue. She shakes her head, the curtain of her hair falling around her face, and snakes her arms around my neck. "Hi."

I smile up at her, slide my hands up her thighs and

plant them at the slight indent of her waist. "Isn't this breaking the rules?"

She's not supposed to be here. I was to experience this weekend without their influence so I could make up my own mind.

"Yes." A wicked grin spills into her dark eyes, sparkling behind the lust. "But I made the rules so I figure I can break them."

"It's good to be queen." I tighten my hold on her, wanting to pull her closer but feeling a little uncertain despite last night.

"Always." She kisses me lightly, an almost chaste touch of lips.

Is she waiting on me to do something more?

My fingers clench against her waist and the muscles of my thighs bunch as her weight shifts in my lap. I want nothing more than to take her in my mouth and lavish her with my tongue. But I need something from her...permission, guidance, a command. I can't do it on my own. Like last night.

She must sense my hesitation because she reaches down and twines her fingers with my own, drawing my hands up to her chest.

"I wanted to check on you." She lifts herself from my lap and slides onto the top of the desk.

She unzips the jacket and I find I'm right. There's nothing beneath the black leather but dirty thoughts and wishful thinking. "Did you masturbate last night after Jacob brought you home?"

My face burns. "No!"

She tilts her head slightly, one eyebrow arching. "What about this morning in the shower?"

My answer is slower this time, but at least I can be honest. "No. I wanted to...I almost did...but I stopped."

Her head falls forward before she looks up at me from beneath the fan of her lashes. Lily brushes her thumb over the pout of my lips. "Good girl." She straightens, bracing a hand on each side of her body. "So none the worse for wear now that the sun is out and reality is knocking on the door instead of hot men in tuxedos?"

I smile at her phrasing and the memory of Jacob and Dylan. "None the worse for wear. I promise."

"I hope you'll think about last night and what it was meant to teach you."

"You mean about trust? Learning to trust you and Jon?"

"It's important you learn to trust us but there's more to it than just that."

"What?"

She sighs, her expression wistful. "That's part of what you have to figure out, Bree. I can't tell you the meaning of the lesson."

I think back to the command I could not follow. Touch yourself.

Why did I hesitate last night?

Even now, I want to reach out and touch Lily. But what if she rejects my advances? I think that's always what I fear will happen. Not that I can't have something...but that I'm not wanted.

Lily lifts herself from the desk and returns to my lap, taking my hands and putting them beneath her jacket. Her hands cover mine and we knead the swell of her breasts until her hands drop and go to the waistband of my jeans.

"Is this what you want to do, Bree?"

Her nipples are tight little pebbles and I cup the weight of her breasts in my palms, grazing the buds with my thumbs. The areola puckers, the flesh drawing tight at the touch and Lily hisses in a breath and says yes beneath her breath.

She unsnaps the button on my jeans and slips her hand into the envelope of space between flesh and fabric.

As her finger finds its target I cut my eyes to the empty corridor. So many opportunities to be brave. So many opportunities to be discovered.

Which will it be, Bree?

My body is so sensitive from last night's adventures, from this morning in the shower. Simply being near Lily, I feel like I'm sitting on a live wire when she touches me. Her mouth plunders mine while her finger swirls around my clit.

Without warning the orgasm crashes over me, tightening things low in my body. Lily swallows my gasp of pleasure beneath her kiss. There's a thrum of current under the surface of my skin, every nerve ending snapping and popping as I drift back down from the ether.

She pulls back slowly, then offers a slow *tsk tsk tsk*, mock disapproval.

"Bad girl, Bree." She lifts her finger to her mouth and licks my arousal from her skin. "You did not ask for permission."

Oh shit.

SURRENDER
CHAPTER ELEVEN

Lily says nothing further about my disobedience before she leaves me alone in the library. While my mind hopscotches around moments of my childhood when I'd been rebuked for the slightest misstep, I can only find an undercurrent of curiosity about what will happen next.

I know before I see the package on my bed that Lily has been in our room. Her scent, heady and exotic, swirls around the space, invading my senses, warming parts still alive with want. The box on my bed is wrapped in a simple white paper with a white ribbon.

I smile.

White.

The color of innocence. After last night I definitely didn't feel very innocent. The experience in the library just now confirms I'm not as prudish as I once thought.

And I did break the rules.

There's a little thrill at being bad. I don't think Lily will hold the infraction against me. The look on her face as she tsked her disappointment said anything but disappointment. She looked...excited.

Did she want me to break the rules? Had she expected it to happen? Maybe it's part of the fun.

I tear into the package on the bed and pull out a pair of fleece pants and a cotton tee. They are snuggly soft but not what I am expecting. I'll admit I'm a little...disappointed. Last night's outfit really pushed the limits of my comfort zone. This is something I'd wear on a typical Saturday night in the dorm.

I guess tonight they want the old Bree.

Dylan and Jacob arrive at the stroke of midnight, although Jacob is careful to keep his hands to himself this time. Has Lily informed him of my infraction? Is this part of my punishment? No more pleasure for me?

We drive past the city limits, the interior of the limo bathed in shifting shadows and light. There's no easy banter tonight. It's not exactly tense between us, but I feel a weight sit next to me and want to shrug it off but I can't figure out how to do that.

I cross and uncross my arms, trying my best to ignore Jacob as much as he's ignoring me. My emotions move from disappointed to aggravated.

Lily is the one who tempted me into breaking the rule. She's the one who showed up looking like sin and salvation in leather. I wipe my sweaty palms on the soft fleece, remembering the softness of her skin. How am I supposed to resist that?

Shouldn't I get some leeway since Lily is the one who provided the opportunity *and* temptation to break the rules?

How could anyone hold out under those circumstances? It's not fair, I pout to myself.

"Don't pout, Gabrielle," Jacob chastises, a smirk tilting up one side of his mouth. His attention remains on the landscape speeding by, his body an advertisement for why men should wear tuxedos more often.

I wiggle in my seat, cross my legs, wipe the pout from my face. "I'm not pouting."

The partition separating the two halves of the vehicle whirs down and I see Dylan studying us in the rear view mirror.

"Is she still pouting?" Dylan's voice fills the darkened interior of the vehicle, a caress against my skin. The man gives good voice.

"Yes." Jacob laughs out the word, twisting his body to switch his attention from the passing landscape to me.

"You might want to tell her she'll regret that, Jacob," Dylan warns. "Then again, I've always had a thing for brats."

Jacob's chuckle deepens. "You *are* a brat, my love."

"Only with you, dear."

"Should we remind her about the rules?"

"There will be time for that later."

I ignore them, irked they are talking about me like I'm not there. I'm irked even more I sort of deserve it.

I am pouting but I'm not sure why. The sense of punishment steals some of the playfulness I've layered over this weekend. I didn't even realize I'd done it. I was serious about exploring a relationship with Jon and Lily. I wanted... something with them. From them.

But what?

I get a sense I'm home when I'm in their arms. It's comfort and acceptance, like they know who I am even if I don't. And yeah, the sex is great.

Last night Dominick said the lessons were about trust. Trusting Lily and Jon. Trusting myself.

But I also had to be worthy of trust and that's when it hits me.

I'd made a promise and I'd not kept it.

Maybe it is a silly promise in the grand scheme of things – ask permission - but it's a promise nonetheless. I'd let them down.

If I want them to be worthy of my trust, I have to be worthy of theirs.

My shoulders drop a little and the weight of disappointment pulls my chin down.

"Don't worry, Bree." Jacob takes my hand and squeezes. "No one expects you to be perfect."

Dylan turns his head slightly and says over his shoulder, "Doesn't mean you won't have to pay for it, though."

The car exits the highway and we follow signs for Masters Winery until we are winding through an extensive orchard. I don't know anything about wine or wine-making but I know the Masters name.

Interesting.

Right past the entrance, there are buildings labeled *gift shop* and *café* and beyond that a halo of outbuildings. Bright halogen lights illuminate the parking lot but as we keep driving, the lights give way to darkness and the occasional street lamp.

Finally, we pull up to a rather non-descript two story building. The dark brick blends into the night at the edges making it hard to determine the size. The only thing that hints to the capacity of the building are the twenty-five or thirty cars in neat lines out front.

Looks like we're going to a party.

A thousand questions bounce around the inside of my skull as I replay last night's encounter. Dominick called me dessert. Am I to be the main course tonight?

I'm not sure how I feel about that. No, scratch that. I'm pretty sure it scares the crap out of me. I'm also fairly turned on if the heat pooling between my legs is any indication.

Dylan and Jacob escort me inside, one on each side. The contrast between the interior and exterior of the building strikes me first as we pass between the rustic, stand alone archway. The inside is as light and airy as the outside is dark and foreboding.

Elegant chandeliers and wall sconces offer soft lighting. Waist high tables with sapphire and white tablecloths dot the floor, candles on mirrored mats giving the room ambiance.

I'm grossly under dressed for the evening, however. The women around me are dressed to the nines – evening gowns in silk and satin with sequins and lace in equal measure. And I'd bet a year's tuition that isn't cubic zirconia sparkling around their necks, wrists, and dangling from their ears. The men are elegantly dressed as well, tuxedos all around.

Several sets of eyes turn in my direction as we step into the room. The looks are ones of interest and appreciation, curiosity, even open lust.

Even the waitstaff is more appropriately dressed than me: bow ties and white gloves, crisp white shirts, pleated pants and pencil skirts.

I hesitate as we pass beneath the arch but Jacob propels me forward. "Don't worry. You'll change."

TRANSFORMATION
CHAPTER TWELVE

W e cut to the right soon after entering the larger party area and step into an office. Dylan takes a folder and a small gift bag from a matronly woman at the door, the bun at the nape of her neck the only thing tighter than the firm line of her mouth. I half expect her to pull out a ruler and smack my hand.

Jacob steers me to a desk in the corner. The room is filled with men and women, most a little older than me, some closer to my age, some I can't tell. They run the spectrum on every level.

It's what they're doing however, that really captures my attention. Their heads are bent, attention intent on something they are reading. I've not seen such concentrated focus since my final in organic chemistry.

"A test?"

Dylan pulls a document from the folder and puts it on the desk. "This is a checklist of all the activities that are theoretically possible for tonight."

I flip through the pages – all eleven of them – my mouth

dropping open a little more as I read some of the items. Some of these I can't even begin to define in my own mind.

Pony play. Luckily it has a big NO written next to it.

Floggers. There's a YES next to this one.

Hmmm.

Jacob flips the document back to page one and points to the first question.

ARE YOU A WILLING PARTICIPANT IN TONIGHT'S EVENT? YES NO

"Jon and Lily are asking for your submission tonight, Bree." The normal playful twinkle in Jacob's eye is replaced with an intense, serious gaze.

I think back to last night with Kylia and Lady V and the explanation I'd been offered of what submission meant for them.

"What does that mean?"

Jacob smiles, as if pleased I'd asked the right question. "Tonight you will give Jon and Lily the power of choosing for you."

Little fingers of dread wrap around my throat. "The power to choose? You mean control?"

Dylan nods. "It is about control. You are giving them control. But it's also about trusting them to use that responsibility wisely, safely, and in a way that gives you both pleasure."

Kenneth said the same thing last night. *Their belief in us is a gift.*

I breathe in, breathe out and do a mental tug of war with myself. I'd given them my trust last night, my belief they would not cause me *harm*.

They didn't let me down. If anyone has reason to doubt

right now, it is them. I'd broken a rule. The only real thing they'd asked of me and I couldn't do it.

Yet they were giving me another chance.

I pick up the pencil and circle YES.

"What will they be choosing for me?"

The matching smirks on Dylan's and Jacob's faces are enough to give me shivers. We spend the next thirty minutes going over the checklist of activities.

At the top in very large, bold letters is the warning:

NO ONE UNDER THE AGE OF 18 IS PERMITTED TO PARTICIPATE IN THESE ACTIVITIES ON THESE PREMISES UNDER ANY CIRCUM-STANCES. FAILURE TO COMPLY RESULTS IN A REPORT TO LOCAL AUTHORITIES AND AN AUTOMATIC LIFETIME GLOBAL BAN FROM ALL MASTERS PROPERTIES.

You'd have to be a hermit not to recognize the Masters name in this town. In addition to several buildings at school which bear their name, not to mention all the scholarships and endowments they fund, they are into real estate, alternative energy, aeronautics, shipping, agriculture... just about every pie there is they have a slice. I even hear they're giving the Tesla dude a run for his money in the race for space.

Anyway, it seems there's more to the Masters' interests than making money. It's good to be rich.

Luckily, the checklist is prefilled otherwise it would take me two hours to read and consider and ask questions.

Dylan and Jacob explain the hard limits that have been assigned: no bestiality, no permanent marks, no body fluids, no humiliation. It scares me a little that some of these must be defined because it means that these things are acceptable for some people.

To each their own, I guess.

When we finally make it through the document, Dylan heads off to turn in my checklist while Jacob presents me with the gift bag. The room around me is empty now; when had the others all left?

I peer inside. "What's this?"

"Tonight's outfit."

The bag is small. I mean...really small. I'm not a big person but there's no way a dress for me is going to fit inside this bag.

"Go on," Jacob prods. "Open it."

I pull out what at first looks like nothing more than leather straps. At the end, however, my brain puts together the puzzle pieces when the silver lock comes into view.

A collar.

Jacob is organizing the rest of the leather into its true form and I see it's basically a thong bikini. In leather. Purple leather, at that.

I smile. Lily has such a wicked sense of humor. It's her fashion sense I'm a little concerned about.

"There's not much here." I pick up the lock, twirl it around my finger. Does it represent another form of control? Is she locking me away?

Jacob picks up the bikini and motions for me to stand. "You'll still be overdressed in this crowd."

I rise to my feet. I don't protest; it's a bikini, not much different than what I would wear to the beach or the pool so it's hard to put up a convincing argument - even with myself - against it.

The collar, on the other hand...

There are screens for privacy and I duck behind one, seeing a row of cubbies against the wall with our names stenciled above. I tuck the sweatsuit in my spot then go about tucking myself into the bikini. There are no mirrors so I can't even tell if I have the thing on correctly but it fits like a swim suit...mostly...so I rejoin the guys.

As Jacob is securing the silver lock around my throat I bristle. At least there's no leash. I've agreed to submit to Jon and Lily's control tonight but the lock makes it feel...different. You lock things in a cage when you don't want them to be free, when you don't want them to escape.

Is that what the collar is meant to tell me? I'm a caged bird in their little world? It doesn't feel right. The lesson doesn't feel like what the *spirit* of the night, or the weekend is supposed to be about.

I shake loose the thoughts.

"Are you ready?"

I nod at Jacob. He hands me a pair of purple heels because of course I need heels in a leather bikini.

"There's a new rule for tonight, Bree."

Oh boy. Dominick told me his rule would last for the weekend so I assume this one will as well. Guilt jabbed at me. I hoped I could do a better job at following this new rule than I did at following Dominick's.

"Tonight, when presented to your dominant, you will assume a kneeling position, arms crossed in front, your forehead resting on your hands."

First the collar, now I'm to prostrate myself? I roll my head around my shoulders, close my eyes. Each step closer to what I want makes it a little more difficult to get it. Why is that? What can this possibly teach me? Why can't we just...be together?

"How do I know who my dominant is?"

"It'll be made clear. You will address your dominant as Sir or Ma'am and speak only when spoken to. Understand."

I nod once then remember Dominick's request last

night to ensure clarity in the parameters for the evening so say aloud. "I understand."

Jacob and I exit the room and the atmosphere has done a one-eighty in the short time we've been inside the office. Oh, the elegant men and women are still there.

Only now they are joined by the men and women who just a short time ago were sitting in the office with me. And like me, they have changed.

For the most part, we're in some state of undress or near undress although I seem to be wearing the most conservative outfit at first glance. My bikini covers most of the important bits.

As we cross the room, Jacob explains in low whispers about cock cages and chastity belts, ball gags and nipple clamps. The man in a diaper with the baby bottle, I'm told, is engaged in age play. There's a woman completely nude but blindfolded being leash-led around by a man in a tux.

Dylan is talking to two exquisite looking women and I breathe a sigh of relief as we join the small gathering. A familiar face. It's a little intimidating, truthfully, to be standing with four fully dressed adults when I'm wearing a leather bikini and my nervousness must show.

"You're quite fetching, Gabrielle," the dark-haired woman says, her voice a seductive and deep purr that seems out of place on the petite frame. Her hair is in an intricate updo, all swirls and curls studded with crystals that catch the light.

She leans her weight back, her left thigh peeking out from the ankle-to-hip slit in the garnet gown. Its bodycon styling and curvy pattern of crystals draw the eye down to the fringed hem and...four-inch fuck-me-pumps.

I snap my eyes back up. Kylia, Kenneth's pet from last night.

I open my mouth to speak but then remember the rules. Kneel. Sir. Ma'am. Is she my dominant? I bite my tongue. Am I allowed to speak? I don't want to disappoint Lily and Jon by breaking another rule.

Fortunately, Dylan senses my confusion. "Right now you're just one of us. You can talk to anyone you wish, however you wish. Although," he waggles a finger in my direction with a playful wink, "I recommend remembering anyone here could be in a position of dominance over you tonight so brattiness is not advisable."

I breathe a sigh of relief at the slight reprieve. "But it can be so much fun."

"For some more than others." I turn and see Kylia's companion is none other than Vivienne. She's wearing a form fitting black mini dress with a sheer lace maxi overlay in sapphire. The color deepens the blue of her eyes, but last night where I saw coolness, tonight I see only heat.

I give Dylan the Girl Scout salute. Or the Boy Scout salute. I can never remember which is which but I hold up three fingers and say solemnly, "I will try and be on my best behavior."

Jacob chuffs. "That ought to last about three minutes."

POWER
CHAPTER THIRTEEN

I shoulder bump him but feel myself blush head to toe, which given my state of dress, is probably obvious to everyone. "I'm open to suggestion. It's hard to give up control to another. I've been on my own for a long time. I'm used to taking care of myself."

A waiter comes by with a tray of canapes while another delivers glasses of white wine. I take a glass but find it filled with sparkling cider instead of the wine I'd expected.

Kylia sips her cider. "Domination and submission are about an *exchange* of power, Bree. Not complete surrender."

I shake my head. "I don't understand the difference."

It's Vivienne who continues. "In submission, the bottom does elevate the desire of the dominant over their own. But the desire of the dominant is the happiness and safety of the submissive."

I let that bounce around my head for a bit as the four of them engage in small talk until Jacob announces we must go. We say our good-byes, but Kylia's eyes promise we'll see each other again.

As we weave through the crowd, a cold shiver scrapes

across my neck. I swivel my head left and right until I find him.

I recognize the type immediately. Spoiled by his position – whether money or job. Plastic smile in a too handsome face. Dishwater blond hair too long to be neat, too short to be pulled into the ridiculous man bun he's fashioned. Surrounded by sycophants hanging on his every word. He's probably never waited for anything in his life.

The look in the half-lowered eyes is not sexual, it's predatory. It's not appreciation, it's covetousness.

It's on the tip of my tongue to tell Jacob but the man loosens the look from his eyes like a dog shaking off fleas. It happens so quickly I think maybe I misinterpreted the look across the room so let it go.

We mix and mingle and I meet new people and greet two more familiar faces. Kenneth and Dominick are in attendance, looking just as handsome in their tuxedos as they did last night in their black on black.

They are both wearing white roses in the lapels of their suit coats and it's then I notice Jacob has one as well. Vivienne is wearing a white rose wrist corsage. Only a few people throughout the room are wearing such adornment and I wonder what it means.

Over the course of the next hour, I have every type of conversation imaginable. With some, we talk BDSM etiquette, and I learn about age play and pony play and about the variety of fetishes on display.

With others, it's the state of the education system or a recent trip to New York or Paris. I'd never visited either city but hopefully after school is finished, I'll find time to travel. It is fun to hear about the museums or exploring cities older than our country.

I excuse myself to find the restroom then worry I won't

be able to get out of the leather outfit without assistance. Luckily another woman sees my distress and offers help. As nervous as I was at the start of the evening, I'm finding it like most mixers I've attended. Some of the partiers just to happen to be wearing leather...or less.

I'm alone when I exit the stall but get all the straps and ties back in place on my own. While washing my hands, I study my reflection in the mirror, seeing myself fully for the first time in the outfit.

My cheeks are flushed. I can't hide the smile. I look... happy? Excited? Whatever Lily and Jon are doing it seems to work. I'm having a good time so I decide not to overthink it too much. There'll be time for that later.

As I'm exiting the bathroom, creepy dude corners me in the hall, bracing an arm on each side of my head to effectively trap me against the wall.

"Who do you belong to?" Beneath the expensive cologne I smell alcohol on his breath so either the party is serving or creepy dude has smuggled in a flask. The plastic smile has melted a touch. He either no longer cares about hiding or he's had too much to drink to effectively don the mask. "I want to negotiate for some of your time tonight."

"My time is spoken for." I go to duck under his arm, but he moves with me and the first prickle of fear snaps to life beneath my skin.

"Sir."

He leans in closer, putting his mouth near the edge of my jaw. At this distance, I can see the dilation of his pupils in the bloodshot eyes. Dude has been imbibing heavily tonight.

"You forgot to call me Sir."

My heart is pounding by this point, adrenaline narrowing my vision to just me and creepy dude. "I also forgot to knee you in the balls but my memory is coming back." I'm pretty sure Jacob and Dylan will back up my brattiness in this situation. Hopefully I won't have to move beyond threats.

Anger slides behind his eyes. So much for hope.

"I'm going to punish you for that."

What happens next happens quickly. One second, he's in my face and the next he's crashing into the wall.

As he crumples to the floor, my vision finally escapes the adrenaline-fueled tunnel. A man steps forward, standing over the fallen form of creepy dude who's trying to untangle his legs from each other.

If I'd thought Dominick formidable, then this guy would make even him take a step back. The scruff darkening a very solid jaw is hours past five o'clock shadow. Instead of dress shoes, he's wearing a pair of well-loved Austin boots in midnight. Alligator, if I'm not mistaken. My dad had a pair just like them. I still have them in storage.

Not even the tux can smooth out the rough edges but an uncut diamond in any form is better than a polished jackass.

"You've been warned before, Keith." A European heaviness sharpens his pronunciation of the words. Images of castles and capes and sexy vampires looking to suck on things flash through my mind.

Keith looks up, his eyes unfocused. "She's here for us to play with, Marcus." He shrugs and gestures in my general direction but avoids meeting my gaze, as if I'm insignificant. "Why else bring such pretty toys to the party."

Marcus flexes his fists, punches them against hips instead of punching Keith. He sighs. "Consider yourself banned, Keith."

Keith finally manages to make his legs work and uses

the wall to push himself upright. "You don't have the keys to the kingdom yet, Marcus." His indignation sounds a lot like whining. "And Masters still needs my bank's connections in Europe."

"Not enough to put up with you assaulting our guests. Leave on your own or I'll remove you."

The man smoothes back the hair loosened from his man bun, tugs on the lapels of his tuxedo jacket. "Where's your private little army?"

"I don't need any help, Keith."

Unlike the disheveled Keith, Marcus doesn't have a hair out of place. Not even the double rose boutonniere on his lapel has lost a petal.

Marcus cuts his head sharply to the left but his eyes never leave Keith. "Would you like to test that theory?"

As Keith storms past Marcus, shoulder checking him on the way out, I release the breath I'm holding and slump against the wall. Marcus is by my side in an instant.

"Are you harmed?" His eyes do a quick assessment but he doesn't touch. I really want him to touch.

I shake my head and inhale deeply, smell the outdoorsy musk of the man mixed with something spicier. "No. A little rattled. Thank you. I think Keith's interest was more whiskey-driven than dangerous."

He takes a step back and sweeps his hand from me to the party. "Let's go find Dylan or Jacob."

"You know them? Do you know Lily and Jon?" I fall in step but he's a foot taller than me, all of it leg, so I'm practically running to keep up. When he realizes this, he slows his pace and matches mine.

"Yes. I work with Lily."

Lily works? I'd never seen her go off to a job, or even talk about a job. I figured her parents were footing the bills which, I'll admit, made me a little jealous at first. It would be nice to have family to support what I wanted in life.

Marcus continues. "I've known Lily for many years."

I'm dreading now what comes next. If they find out about Keith... "Any chance we could pretend this didn't happen? I don't want to ruin the party and they've gone to a lot of trouble. I'm not –"

Marcus stops abruptly and spins. His hand comes up and cups my elbow, the gesture completely platonic. He leans down and I'm swimming in the seductive darkness in his eyes. "You are definitely worth it, Bree."

There's some serious eye contact and I'm lost in the sincerity of his words. The moment is brief. He clears his throat, lowers his hand.

"I can't hold this information back. I would never forgive myself if the rest of your evening was anything but what Lily planned."

Wait? He knows about Lily's plans?

"What does she have planned?"

We're walking again and he ignores my question. Jacob and Dylan see us, the relaxed smiles turning serious in an instant. They meet us halfway across the floor.

I pre-empt the questions with, "It's nothing."

"It wasn't nothing," Marcus counters just as quickly. "Keith took liberties –" Jacob's face gets red. Dylan's fists clench and he mutters a few choice words.

"That were stopped before they went anywhere," I finish. "I've been to frat parties. I know how to handle someone like Keith."

Jacob pulls a cell phone out of an inside jacket pocket. "I'm going to call Lily."

"No." I pluck the phone from his grasp.

"No?" He and Dylan echo. Marcus merely looks amused.

He crosses his arms and leans back on his heels. The motion makes his biceps strain the fabric of the jacket and I pause a moment to see if the coat or his muscles will win the battle. Unfortunately it's the coat but it's a close call.

I shake away the wandering lust and pull my thoughts back to my own test of wills. "Jacob, you told me the first night your job was gatekeeper, protector. Do I look harmed or hurt?" He shakes his head. "I understand you want to tell her, but don't let it ruin the evening because someone got mouthy." After a few seconds, I hand him back the phone and add, "Please. Let the evening continue."

It's become important to me to continue this weekend. Not just because of how much I want to explore a relationship with Lily and Jon. But because I'm discovering things about myself. I'm finding out who I am. I don't know all the answers yet. Hell, I'm not even sure of all of the questions. I hadn't realized how much of myself I'd lost over the years.

Dylan and Jacob share a look and I can tell before they turn their attention back to me, I've won the argument.

"Alright," Jacob agrees. "If you're sure. I still want to tell Lily."

"I agree." I turn to Marcus who has maintained a silent presence during our talk. "Will you call her, explain what happened?" Marcus is concerned for my well-being but detached enough to present the information in a balanced way. "Let her know the situation is handled and I'm no worse for wear."

Marcus nods and turns to Dylan. "I've got to make sure Keith is off the premises. Can you..." He sighs heavily and cuts his eyes quickly to me.

Dylan perks up. "Sure thing. I'm sorry, man."

Marcus inclines his head as he shakes hands with Dylan then walks away and because I can, I watch him. The man does something to a pair of pants. If we met under different circumstances, would I … I stop the thought. I'm not normally the type.

Wait. I look around. Look down at the leather bikini I've poured my body into for the night. The collar around my neck. I touch the little lock holding the collar in place.

Maybe I am the type.

The lights blink and a murmur rises over the crowd. A few people closest too me actually clap their hands and squeal like children getting candy.

"What's that mean?" I look to Dylan and Jacob.

Dylan lowers his gaze, biting his lower lip briefly. It's a gesture both boyish and seductive and I'm intrigued by the mischievousness lurking in his grin. He responds, "It means the party's just getting started."

EXHIBITION
CHAPTER FOURTEEN

The party, it turns out, is a charity auction to support a local domestic abuse shelter and a veteran's rehab facility in town. I've heard Lily mention both now that I think about it but never paid much attention. I'm ashamed at that. I don't know enough about her. Only surface things. On the other hand, she seems to have figured out my darkest secrets, my secret desires.

Jacob is walking with me to the stage and through the crowd I can see that others who have assumed a submissive role like myself are standing off to the side. Some look excited. Some look terrified.

"Uhh...what is being auctioned tonight?" But I know the answer before Jacob says, "You."

The word silences me and the gears in my head start churning out excuses on why I can't do this. Why I shouldn't do this.

There's a room full of people here tonight I don't know.

I've already discovered one asshole in the crowd. Who says there aren't more?

I'm wearing a fucking leather bikini.

The thought of walking out on that stage in the leather bikini churns my stomach like it's spawned a tornado.

But it's what going on in my sex that focuses my attention. I'm wet. I can tell – the leather doesn't leave much to the imagination. It hugs and cups and touches you in places like a lover.

I never thought I'd use a word like quiver but I'm damn near vibrating inside my body at the thought of what will happen on that stage. Standing in front of all these people in damn little except good intentions.

I'm about as far from an exhibitionist as you can get. I prefer the shadows. I prefer being unknown. It's safer.

But tonight I am not Bree, the invisible.

Tonight, I am Gabrielle.

WWGD?

What would Gabrielle do?

I have no clue. But I guess I'm about to find out.

Jacob leaves me with the matron from the office who ensures she has my checklist from earlier. She puts me fourth in line then goes to receive other auctionees for the event.

I take a moment to look at the others up for auction. The man in front of me is nude except for a cock cage around his very impressive cock. The woman behind me is nude except for the collar and leash bisecting her ample breasts.

I feel a little over dressed and have to laugh at the turn. Under-dressed when I walked in. Over-dressed now.

The lights blink again a few minutes later and it's as if someone turns off the volume for the crowd. The lights dim, black silk curtains fall from the ceiling to drape the perimeter and electric candles on the walls and tables flare to life.

The change in ambiance is immediate and pervasive.

In the few minutes I've been occupied at the front of the room, the tables have been pushed to the side and a variety of equipment has been spread around the room. Padded sawhorses. Long tables with cuffs at both ends. Against the wall there's a rather large X-shaped contraption that boggles the mind.

A spotlight hits the stage and an exquisite looking emcee sashays to the center. I don't try and guess their gender. They are both and neither, taking the best of both and melding it into an art form.

The shoulder length hair is layered in a shag that wouldn't work on anyone else. Neither would the platinum but on them…sheer perfection against the rich mahogany of their skin.

The makeup is flawless, an intricate pattern of sparkles and glitter in red, pinks, and yellows highlighting the eyes. Finely arched eyebrows lift in amazement and ridiculously long lashes tipped in glitter flutter as they welcome the applause rippling across the crowd.

They are wearing the most outrageously interesting outfit I've seen outside of Pinterest. A snug tailored jacket in white, the wide silk lapels embroidered with tiny birds fluttering from a cage. The tails of the jacket flare out at the hips into a long train of tulle bedazzled with thousands of crystals that catch the soft light. White harem pants, also bedazzled with sequins and crystals, and clear mules finish the outfit.

They walk like they own the moment. They do.

"Hello Sirs and Madams and Gentlethems!" they sing to the crowd. "You are lookin' very fine tonight. All dressed up and no one to beat. Let's change that!"

The crowd cheers and laughs.

"I'm River for those that are new tonight." River does a bow then half curtsey as applause again ripples through the crowd. "Thank you, thank you. The rules are the same as with any other night here at Masters. If you don't buy, you don't touch without permission." He gives them an impish grin but there's serious warning in the finger that skims over the crowd. I've seen firsthand how serious they take their guests' protection and I'm relieved to know Keith is truly a one-off.

River continues, strutting from one end of the stage to the other. They swish their hips and send the tulle train cascading over the raised dais to blanket a gentleman standing near the stage. He throws a kiss up to River who catches it one-handed, brings it to their lips and then licks the air kiss from their fingertips. The crowd loves it.

I have to admit, River is quite the player and I envy the comfort they derive from the attention.

They hold up the folder I'd seen the matron checking earlier. "All limits will be respected. Our dungeon master was called away on an emergency but Leo...wave to the crowd Leo."

A rather bookish looking accountant complete with black framed glasses - and a double rose boutonniere - steps forward and waves his hand and bows to River then to the crowd.

"Leo is making the rounds and he has his dungeon monitors set up around the room. They are noted by white rose boutonnieres and wrist corsages. If anyone needs assistance, go to a monitor."

River drops their chin and affects a rather serious looking pout. "Anyone breaking the rules has to deal with me tonight and you do not –" foot stomp –"want to make me mess up my makeup tonight people."

The serious face is replaced in the space of a heartbeat with the more playful River with a quick snap-snap-snap of their fingers. "Minimum bids have been set at two tokens and halfsies and quarters are welcome. You all know our charities for tonight. Let's get started." Their voice rumbles out, dropping to a sexy bass then pitching back to the tenor on a long last syllable.

"Our first player tonight..."

A steady hum of conversation slides over the crowd as the first young woman steps onto the stage. She's old hat at this, I can tell. She preens and moues for the audience with practiced ease, sliding her hands up the side of her chest to amplify her breasts before spinning around to give them a saucy wiggle of her bare ass. The bidding quickly escalates up to four and a half tokens before River declares a winner.

An impressed ooooo from the woman behind me turns my head. "What is a token worth?"

"Ten."

It's for charity and the people here look like they can afford to be generous if the diamonds sparkling are any indication. I don't know if the house last night belonged to either of the fearsome foursome, but someone is doing well for themselves.

Still, forty-five bucks for charity seems a little cheap given what they get for the money.

"Hopefully they'll round up to an even fifty bucks for a good cause," I say out loud, hoping there's no one close that will make me regret the sarcasm.

The woman snorts. "Honey, ten *thousand* per token."

What the actual fuck?

My face must give away my disbelief because she nods. "I know, right? I just hope I go above minimum. I saw one guy last year go for seven tokens. Two old dommes got into a bidding war over him. He had a cock like an angry bull though. I guess they wanted to relive a little of the glory days. Can't say I blame them." She polished her nails against her bare shoulder. "Wow."

The next two bids go quickly, three and three-and-a-quarter tokens. And then it's me. The woman behind pokes me and nods excitedly toward the stage but my feet won't budge.

Any earlier bravado has run its course. I'm picturing myself in those snuggle white fleece pants and cotton tank, cozied up in my bed, a pint of ice cream in one hand and the remote in the other.

"It looks like our newb is feeling a little shy." River practically dances on the toes of their sequined-slippered feet toward me and holds out a hand. "Come on, darlin'. We were all virgins at one point." They cock their hip and stage whisper to the crowd, "Well, everyone except Jacob. He was born a slut."

I slip my hand in River's, letting them lead me on to the dais. I avoid looking out to the audience and instead focus on not tripping over my own shadow. My heart is thundering and sweat beads in the small of my back, leaving a chill on my skin.

"Do I have an opening bid?"

"Three!" Dylan steps forward, a proprietary gleam darkening his California good looks.

Immediately a woman shouts, "Three-and-a-half!" followed by another female voice, this one familiar "Four!"

I swivel my head to see Kylia moving through the crowd to stand at the front of the room.

I get lost in the proprietary lust lighting behind those dark eyes. So different than the pet who knelt by Kenneth's side, contained herself in nearly every way. This is not a woman to be contained.

Another two bidders join in and when my attention finds the auction again, they are eight tokens. Wait? Eight?

Eight.

Dylan and Kylia have found each other at the front of the room, whispering conspiratorially as River starts the final countdown on eight tokens to some stranger. He's handsome enough. We'd talked for a few moments during Jacob's tour around the room. Intelligent. Funny. Nice enough. But not...

"Ten." Dylan and Kylia make the announcement together and a ripple of gasps and ohs skitter across the room.

"My, oh my!" River shimmies around me, the tulle train making a puddle at my feet. "This is a record, my lovelies. Going-" -snap- "going-" -snap- "gone!" Snap.

And just like that. I've been sold.

My mind knows it's figurative. More like a short term rental. Looking at Kylia and Dylan as they bask in the applause and appreciative smiles, I wonder if the congratulatory remarks are for the generous donation or for the prize.

Things get fuzzy as I'm led away from the dais. There's a high pitched ringing in my ears and my vision has tunneled to the small space where my feet will land. It's amazing the amount of concentration it suddenly requires to put one foot in front of the other.

Dylan and Kylia are one on each side, book ends, supporting columns and even though we are all approximately the same height I feel small in comparison. When I finally pull my gaze up, I realize the crowd has parted and we are walking three abreast down the center aisle created.

They look hungry, enthralled. A leering Roman crowd as the sacrifice is led to the arena. The three of us enter a largish room. How large is hard to say. Shadows play along the walls from the corner sconces and the overhead lights are a series of concentric circles shooting diffused light toward the ceiling.

Music creates an undercurrent in the dark. A pounding bass. A gentle play of notes over it. Hard and soft. Harmonious together.

As my eyes adjust and I turn back to find Dylan and Kylia standing side by side, watching me intently. I'm back to feeling like the sacrifice in the lion's den, the center of attention. Awareness prickles along my exposed skin – and in this outfit there's a lot of that – and a shudder ripples through my body.

"Wh—" I bite back the word out of habit more than anything. Resentment is a bitter taste on my tongue. Rules. There are rules that I'm supposed to be following. What are they? Fuck if I know.

Oh yeah. Only speak when spoken to. My subconscious remembered this one. I'd grown up being a silent member of my cobbled-together family. A performing monkey for my aunt and uncle to show how wonderful they were for taking in their orphaned niece.

But this is not then.

And I am not that girl.

REQUEST
CHAPTER FIFTEEN

I'm here because I want to be. And I'm here with people who've given me no reason to doubt them.

My knees wobble a bit as I drop to the floor, palms pressing into the thick, luxurious rug. At least I won't be uncomfortable while I prostrate myself. I lean forward, close my eyes, and press my forehead against the backs of my hands.

Every sensation is magnified tenfold. The tickle of my hair against my cheek. The way my fingers curl into the plush of the carpet beneath me. The thrust of my ass high above the rest of me. The heat of arousal between my legs.

I sense Dylan and Kylia move to stand behind me and open my eyes. There's a slight roar in my ears, like listening to the world underwater so I swallow hard and still the noises in my head.

"Good girl."

A hand caresses my backside. Judging by the size I'd say it has to be Dylan. He cups the bare curve of my ass, traces the line of leather where the thong circles my waist but he doesn't go where my body needs him to go. I suck in a breath and let out a moan.

"Oh, listen to that Dylan." The tips of Kylia's toes come into the limited circle of my vision. She's removed the fuck-me-pumps and stands in her bare stocking feet. "Our little sub sounds frustrated."

"I don't know why." Dylan gives me a light swat and I yip with surprise. "A little birdie told me she got off in the library earlier today."

A little birdie? More like a Bird of Paradise, I think. Silently of course. I have a feeling I'm in enough trouble without my mouth digging a deeper hole. You know those laughs that say something isn't funny? Yeah...that's what Kylia does. A hoarse chuckle much too deep for her diminutive frame. She tunnels her fingers through my hair, tangles her fingers at the nape and pulls my head back.

Our eyes meet – hers wide and bright even in the low light. "That was not allowed, Bree. Naughty." She leans closer. The familiar fragrance of orchids and the homey aroma of vanilla swirl around her. "Naughty."

"I'm— ow!"

The apology dies on my lips when Dylan smacks my ass, no playful tap this time. "Kylia, do you remember asking Bree a question?"

Rebellion blossoms like the fading sting of the swat.

"No. I don't."

There's another sharp crack against the bare back of my thigh but I suck in rather than cry out. A tightness curls around my stomach, fills up my chest, burns at the back of my eyes. But I stay quiet.

Because I want more.

"Seems like she can learn from her mistakes though."

Kylia tugs gently on my hair, urging me to stand. She

and I are eye to eye, toe to toe. Her long black hair is pulled back, not a hair escaping from the tight bun. Like they would dare!

"Do you remember your safeword, Bree?"

I nod, hesitant to speak but she has spoken to me directly so I add quickly, "Yes, ma'am."

Kylia leads me forward. My heart speeds up a little as I glance around the room. I wait to see Lily and Jon appear as they did the last time, but nothing. What if they're not there?

Kylia stops and I shake myself from the path of my thoughts to avoid running into her.

They're near. I choose to believe. But it's a hard choice.

We're standing before a large cabinet. I don't know how I missed it before. Inlaid into the massive doors is some kind of carved artwork and once my eyes adjust and I can focus on the detail, I see it is people in various positions of supplication, some being spanked or whipped, others worshipping the figure before them. A few of the groupings involve sex and my body shows me it's tuned in to the moment even if my mind is a little far away.

Dylan opens the doors and reveals a...bondage shopping extravaganza. Whips, floggers, and paddles in a dozen different sizes. Each. Cuffs - leather, fur-lined, you name it. Enough rope to scale a small mountain. Hairbrushes. Wooden spoons. Even a pair of flip flops. And those are the things I recognize. Half the stuff I've never seen before.

A dozen images flash behind my eyes on what could be done with all of that and I squeeze my legs tight to keep the interest from dripping down my thighs.

Dylan's propped himself up against the open door, arms crossed. "I think she's curious about our little toy rack, Ky. Should we let her get a closer look?"

The leash drops down the line of my spine and Kylia motions with her hand. "Much closer. Why don't you pick one, Bree?"

Great, I think. Silently because I know better at this point. I get to be the instrument of my own demise. But I remember Lily's rules. I am in charge.

I step up to the rack and study the implements, immediately taking whips out of the picture. The memory of a western I saw once where the cowboy uses a whip to spur a horse to jump over a cliff comes to mind. The paddles bring to mind naughty school girls and while I won't mind exploring that little fantasy at some point - Lily will be an excellent stern headmistress - the flat wooden surface has holes drilled in to it to cut down on wind resistance. Too much thought has gone into making that.

Instead, my eye jumps to a purple cascade of leather. I run my fingers through the soft fall of supple cowhide, amazed at the caress over my skin. The grip is braided and fits like it was made for my hand. The fact that it's about nine inches long tells me the maker is either incredibly obtuse or a genius. I go with genius.

"I think she's chosen." Dylan holds out his hand and I put the device in his palm. He wraps his fingers around the leather handle, and intimate caress, and closes his eyes momentarily beneath the weight of some memory. There are lusty things going on behind his eyes when he looks at me again. "One of my favorite floggers."

Kylia walks behind him, draping her arm over his shoulder and resting her cheek against the back of her hand. She murmurs into his ear but keeps her eyes on me. "It's going to be a good night, Dylan. Get her ready."

"Yes, ma'am."

Dylan pulls out a set of fur lined cuffs and secures them

around my wrists and ankles then leads me to an odd contraption in the corner. It looks a little like a hobby horse without the head. The body is angled downward and on each side are smaller risers. A thick cushion covers the entire thing and when Kylia directs me into position me on the device, my legs straddling the body, I learn why. My torso is draped over the center platform with my ass high in the air.

Dylan clicks the cuffs to the four corners and I'm effectively on display, ass up. I pull against the restraints, more out of habit than fear. The cuffs don't give and the fur and cushion beneath my knees and stomach prevent any real discomfort.

I'm trapped but the adrenaline that floods my body and heats my blood is not fight or flight. It's excitement.

"It's the best feeling in the world, Bree," Dylan laughs but it's not a question so I'm not allowed to answer. He plays his fingers over the cuff at one wrist. "Like being held by someone you love. And wait until you hit subspace the first time." The sound he makes is hungry, desperate. "I can't explain what it's like."

Kylia's hand cups my bottom then snakes between my thighs, tracing the lines of the leather thong I still wear. I want her - someone, anyone - to reach beneath that leather and touch me where I need to be touched.

Dylan is standing near my head when he says, "I think she likes it." But my attention is all for Kylia and her hands.

Dammit. I wish they would talk to me. Words are crowding on my tongue. No. *Yes*. Please. *More*.

"Of course, Lily did tell us tonight is about reminding Bree of the rules."

Rules? The rules say I'm in charge and I say Kylia needs

to keep doing what she was doing. I'm so revved up at this point I groan when she pulls her hand away.

The door behind us clicks open and I turn my head to see Marcus standing by the door, his impossibly large frame pushing back the darkness. He says nothing but his eyes find me immediately. His chin drops a notch and then he rolls his head slightly. But again, his eyes never leave mine.

A slap to my right butt cheek brings my attention back to Dylan and Kylia. "The dungeon master is just checking to see if bad girls are where they need to be."

Kylia hands Dylan a gauzy length of purple chiffon. "Let's make sure her attention stays focused. I wouldn't want her to miss the object lesson tonight."

While Dylan secures the blindfold, I struggle to hold still and puzzle out Kylia's words.

What lesson am I supposed to be learning? That I can get impossibly turned on by parading around a room full of strangers in less than I wear to bed most nights in the privacy of my own bedroom? That the thought of strangers desiring me enough to spend tens of thousands of dollars spikes my self-confidence? That one stranger in alligator boots has taken up space in my thoughts?

That disappointing Lily and Jon by breaking the rules has me worried they'll soon toss me aside like a toy once favored but now forgotten?

I hear the door click open again but can't look this time.

"She's thinking, ma'am." Dylan brushes a lock of hair off my forehead then moves away. "I can hear the wheels spinning."

Kylia tuts. "Then give her something to take her mind off her thoughts, Dylan."

"Yes, ma'am."

The first smack catches me just under the curve of my left butt cheek.

"Ow!" I complain before remembering the rules. Damn it.

"Bree." My chin is tipped back with a finger beneath my jaw and I feel a cheek, soft and feminine, press against my own. My name breathes against my ear several more times. Something exotic and floral swirls in my nostrils but there's no hint of vanilla bringing me back home. I think of forbidden desires and dark fantasies. "We need to work on your self-control."

The next five smacks came in a quick flurry, the heat blossoming just beneath the pain threshold but spreading like a slow burn between my thighs. My nipples are hard nubs scraping the inside of the leather bra, like steel against flint. The spark ignites new ribbons of fire throughout my body.

One fire, in particular, I try to deal with by grinding against the wooden support between my thighs. I'm rewarded with a sharper smack this time, the sting more pronounced against my already warm flesh.

"I know you want to come, Bree." A female voice rasps in my ear, first one side, then moves to the other, connecting my heart to the want swirling around. "I know you want to ease that ache inside."

There are so many empty places inside of me wanting to be filled, but right now one is center stage.

"Yes." I hate how easily I give in to the want but it's a greedy thing. It feeds on the hands roaming my flesh, wanting to capture them, hold them still until they scratch the itch pulsing beneath the surface.

"Do you want me inside your body?" A male voice this time.

I've tasted what it's like to feel the rush of pleasure as it drowns my senses and I want more. If I can't be loved, than being desired is a close second.

I bite my lower lip between my front teeth, but the admission pushes through. "Yes."

Someone is standing directly in front of me now. The blindfold hides the details but the gooseflesh that comes to life tells me it's male.

Two hands cradle my face and the shadow deepens as it grows larger. A slow exhale of breath. The swipe of a tongue across my bottom lip. The kiss devours my mouth, tastes me so deeply and completely I'm not sure I remember to breathe until he pulls back and I hear the rasp of his own ragged breathing.

"What will you do for it?"

My confession is instant. "Anything." And I would. I'd crawl. I'd beg this time without hesitation.

"Then you should have called me sir."

DENIAL
CHAPTER SIXTEEN

The failure sweeps over me, cold and heavy, and I drown beneath the tumble of emotion.

The kneeling bench is silently but swiftly adjusted and suddenly I'm standing. My wrists are still cuffed but my hands stretch over my head, drawing my torso into a long taut line. My ankles are released and the sudden freedom is more unnerving than the prior constraint. Is this where they tell me if I can't follow the rules I can go live...play... elsewhere? I widen my stance, but go statue still. I don't want to run. I want to belong here. With someone.

With them.

But I've broken their rules.

Again.

Is this where they release me, tell me to leave? It's what I expect, why I've avoided any situation that would give someone else this power over my life. If there's no one I want, then there's no one to miss when they go away. And if I don't give anyone the chance to want me, then they can't send me away when they get bored or disappointed.

"It was expected, Bree."

The voice in my ear is soft and feminine. I know this voice, heard it whisper my name, cry out in passion. A mouth presses against my ear, nuzzles the little hollow just behind the shell.

"A mistake. Two mistakes. Three mistakes."

A hand curls around my hip, snakes up my stomach between my breasts to the little clasp holding the spiderweb of leather straps in place. With a flick, the leather thong falls away leaving me bare.

At their mercy.

I tuck my chin against my shoulder, try and steady the thready pulse tightening around my throat. I swallow back the tears burning behind the blindfold.

"We all make them." Someone tall and broad-shouldered spoons me from the back, his bulk a comforting presence. "It's what we do afterward that counts."

My earlier rebellion crawls away, overshadowed by a desire to make amends. As a kid I'd been too scared to cross the boundaries. As an adult, I hadn't let anyone else set boundaries for me. Lily had drawn a line in the sand then given me the chance to walk across.

Was she showing me I can step back? Without fear.

"And being with people that won't hold them against us."

Without enmity.

"No matter the mistake."

"But not without punishment." There's a playful nip at the corner of my mouth.

I know I'm about to pay a price, and likely a painful one, for my earlier disobedience, but the weight that settles over me is not fear or apprehension.

It's peace.

I'm not sure how that's possible and I have to stifle the giggle that bubbles up.

I hear a whooshing sound behind me, a disturbance of the air that hums beneath the pulse of music I hadn't noticed playing before. A deep bass thrums and my heart falls into rhythm with it.

A kiss whispers against my lips. "Breathe in."

The first thud of the flogger against my buttock is heavy and intimate. It hugs the curve of my cheek, gives a lick around the hip bone, a taste between my thighs. Holy hell. The leather falls again and again, thrumming in syncope to the music and my heart and the new pulse that is throbbing between my legs.

As steady as the kiss of the leather is the voice reminding me to breathe but it fades into the long tunnel of desire and arousal. Hands tweak my nipples, dip between my slit to the swollen ache to capture my desire and bring it to my own lips for me to taste, savor.

I'm dancing on the edge of orgasm but I will myself back. They have not given permission. And I will not let my body disobey them.

The sensations steal me away from the four walls of the room. Leather on flesh, flesh on flesh, longing and want. Mistakes and forgiveness. Forgiveness and acceptance.

My world narrows down. The flogger. Lips against mine. Fingers on my body. Breathy words in my ear. The music carries it all, lifts it up, brings it forward and back, delivers it with darkness and light.

I cry out and sag against the cuffs but before my body sinks too low strong arms sweep me upward. My hands are freed in the same instant and I curl into a chest broad enough to carry the world. Words are whispered. Encouragement. Appreciation. Support.

I wrap them around me, the words, the bodies, feeling safe. Lily promised to push me to the edge and she'd done just that. Let me make mistakes. Several of them. I'd had to learn the lesson the hard way, though, and they taught it well. It was ok to fail. It was not ok to run away from it.

I am done running.

FULFILLMENT

BOOK THREE

MASTERED BY DEGREES

Fulfillment

DAYDREAM
CHAPTER ONE

The next morning, my body still feels like it belongs to someone else. I can't explain the floaty feeling that carried me away last night after I collapsed. It was a near state of unconsciousness, a type of blissful comfort. Flying high one moment, drifting the next, finally buoyed by the solid warmth of Jon and Lily. Their hands. Their voices. Their bodies.

When I finally pulled my senses together, I reached for them but found Kylia and Dylan spooned around me. A blanket smelling of orchids and fresh linen was tucked tightly to my chin which was good because they'd mistaken the shivers for a chill rather than disappointment. The drop had been as precipitous as the rise.

Kylia stayed with me a bit after I got home. We didn't talk, talking seemed too much effort. Besides, all I'd wanted to do was crawl in bed.

I woke to clouds. Stormy. Grey. Roiling. Good. It's a mirror for my own attitude. The dorm is quieter than normal with the holiday, even the people who've stayed for the weekend parties have abandoned campus for alternative sleeping arrangements until school resumes on Tuesday. I want to be lazy. I have nothing to do. No one to do it with. Another regular day in the life of Gabrielle Fontenot.

Lucky me.

I'm pouting. I know it. Lily told me I wouldn't see them but the little tastes of their presence throughout the weekend so far made me hope they would be more active. After last night...my body remembers every touch, every kiss of leather and lips. Heat starts to curl lazily in my belly, a twist of want and denial tugging between my breasts and my pussy.

I muffle the *arrgghh* of frustration in my pillow.

If I'm not careful, I'm going to do something I'll regret so I push out of my grumpiness, grab my shower bucket, and death-march to the bathroom.

As I walk the empty hall, I make a mental list of things I can do today. Practical: study for the statistics test, laundry, pull an extra shift at the computer lab. Lazy: movie, junk food, nap.

Nothing appeals to me. My body is restless.

Inside the communal bathroom, I head to my now-favorite shower and slap back the curtain on the last stall, the metal rings making an angry swish across the bar that echoes against the ugly green tile.

Taped to the showerhead is an envelope, a large B scrawled on the outside in a familiar handwriting.

I open it and find a business card with an address. The note reads:

Good morning sweetness.

Jon and I wanted so much to comfort you

last night. There is a method to our madness. I promise.

If I know you (and I do) your fingers are twitching for something to do. Go to the address on the card and ask for Thiago. He'll help you feel better.

I trace the 'L' scrawled across the bottom then bring the paper to my nose, breathe in the scent of orchids, the scent of Lily.

I tuck the note away for safekeeping and shower quickly. Temptation is shoved aside out of curiosity.

Back in the room I map out the address on the bus schedule taped to my closet door. I take the bus everywhere and I know my usual routes by memory, but this place is in the Garden District. That's the swanky part of town. Not my usual stomping grounds. It's several transfers away and will take an hour or so to get there but I don't care.

I dress without thought: my favorite jean shorts, a cami and button down. The days are still warm in New Orleans this time of year although nights by the river can be cooler. I grab my backpack and head downstairs, pushing open the doors with a heave only to stop in my tracks.

Jacob leans against the back bumper of the Towncar from our ride share a few days ago, his impossibly long legs stretched out and crossed at the ankles. He lowers the book propped in one hand, letting his eyes do an unapologetic linger on my legs. His smile makes me forget about the grey clouds.

"Good morning, Bree." Jacob pushes off the car with his hips and opens the back door. "I understand you're going to see Thiago today." He does a little caterpillar dance with his eyebrows and looks at me beneath lids hooded with knowledge and dark thoughts. "Lucky you."

I slow step toward the car but point to the front. "I'd rather sit in the front if you don't mind." Sitting in the back when it's just the two of us seems more pretentious than I can pretend. "If it's stuffed with fast food wrappers and cheap novels, I promise not to laugh."

He does an easy pivot, closing the back door with one hand while opening the front with the other. "My novels are never cheap."

I scoot in next to copies of Influence: The Psychology of Persuasion and Dare to Lead, along with several Darynda Jones and TJ Klune novels, two of my favorite authors.

"Quite the range." I nod to the books now sitting in my lap when Jacob slides behind the wheel, bringing the engine to life before relieving me of the books. His knuckles skim my thighs, and the little zip of familiarity warms my cheeks and places lower on my body.

He twists in the seat to set the books behind him, the crisp white shirt stretching taut across obliques and abs I'd kill to see. "My job involves a lot of waiting, so I can either play Words with Friends on my phone or read."

"I kill at Words with Friends."

He peeks at me over the rim of his sunglasses, those impossibly dark brown eyes twinkling if such a thing is possible, as we merge into traffic on Jefferson Highway. "Challenge accepted."

We fill the short drive with talk of books and school. Jacob is in the MBA program at Loyola and chats easily about plans for his own series of high-end wine and bourbon tasting clubs after graduation. He is more circumspect when it comes to his current work life.

"I work for the Masters Corporation."

Masters. The name dripping all over the property we visited last night, as well as a foundational family in the New Orleans area. The city leaders offered to rename the Superdome after the family because of their charitable contributions in the wake of Hurricane David a few years ago but the family declined.

I cross my legs, angling my body more toward Jacob, pleased when his eyes follow the movement. I'd never been one to think I could use sexuality as a lure but apparently the last two evenings have more of an impact than I anticipated.

Lily isn't one to talk about herself much. Maybe I can get Jacob to get more information.

"They must be super lenient bosses to let you and Lily use their private cars and invite poor unknown college students to their parties."

"I've worked for the family for ten years and have known them much longer. I get a certain amount of freedom."

"Does Lily work for them as well?"

He worries his bottom lip between his teeth, using a lane change to put off answering my question while he maneuvers the car across several lanes of traffic. "Yes," he answers finally. "She does."

I wait for more, then laugh a little at the brevity of his response. "Is that all I get?"

He leans to the right until his elbow rests on the center console. "That's all you get from me. If you want to know more, you should ask Lily."

I want to know more. Lots more. Everything in fact. Lily and I have been roommates for more than a year and talk in the rare moments we aren't in class. She spends most weekends off campus while I hide in the library between work shifts, however, so our paths don't cross often.

But when they do, she intrigues me. She is calm where I am nervous. She is confidant where I am insecure. She is sexy in raggedy sweats or slinky leather pants with peek-a-book tops.

I am Switzerland.

And she can talk about anything or be comfortable in silence. Often, I lose myself watching her over the top of a book. She has more pillows than IKEA piled on her bed and usually curls on top of them like a contented feline, her hair a messy knot mystically attached to her head.

Lily has everything from Dr. Who to Daffy Duck on the soft harem pants she usually wears around the dorm. She favors Finders Keepers and Tory Burch but has enough Gucci and Prada to be impressive. There're a few leather pieces as well, sex and sin waiting to be defined by her body.

Yes, I peeked through her closet. I'm not proud of it. Sometimes I need to wrap the sensual scent of her - linen and orchids and something I just think of as Lily - around me.

ALLEGORY
CHAPTER TWO

By the time I pull my head out of my fantasy world, we are pulling into a gated drive. I immediately recognize the place. The Saint-Domingue House, a New Orleans landmark famous for its first owner, Pierre Lafitte, the pirate Jean Lafitte's younger brother. Apparently even then a blacksmith could own a ten-acre estate, and no one would question where he got the funds.

I look to Jacob as we pull beneath the line of massive southern live oaks. The magnificent alley of trees is renowned in the city for their beauty and the mystical way they'd survived multiple hurricanes over the years. "Are we doing a tour?"

The place had been bought and sold over the decades since it was built in the early nineteenth century, but the current owner picked it up at a low point in the seventies and turned it into the beauty it was today. Butterfly gardens, a dozen fountains, and several koi ponds dot the massive estate.

The house and grounds are a favorite small venue destination for brides and old New Orleans money. It's Sunday, certainly a busy day on the calendar especially given the holiday weekend. But the place looks empty. We pull in next to a sleek red Audi in the private parking area directly behind the main house.

"The house is closed today." Jacob parks then jumps out, coming around to my side to open the door. "Thiago will meet you in the foyer."

My nerves tingle to life, the rational part of my brain desperately trying to tamp down the heat already pooling in my belly and between my legs.

Remember the rules.

Whatever the day holds with Thiago, I know an orgasm isn't in my future. The note said Thiago would make me feel better about my restlessness. Since I doubt we'll be working up a sweat, maybe it will be a relaxing private tour of the beautiful house and gardens. There are worse ways to spend a day, but in truth, disappointment flutters inside at the vanilla prospects.

I tug the backpack higher on my shoulder, once again feeling underdressed as I walk slowly up the manicured path. My shorts have frayed edges, an old pair of jeans I'd used for chem lab. I'm sure the acid washing I did wasn't what the fashion gods had in mind, but they are comfortable.

The path spills me onto the two-story veranda where a red door waits. I feel a little like Alice in Wonderland but no white rabbit jumps from the bushes. I don't know if I should walk in or knock so I go with caution and raise my hand, but the door opens, and I'm greeted by a man I can only call distinguished.

He's standing ramrod straight, and not even the slight pot belly pushing at the buttons of his expensive suit detract from the air of quiet authority.

"Ms. Fontenot. Welcome to the Saint Domingue house. I'm Thiago Romero."

Mr. Romero - only his surname will do after meeting him - ushers me inside and I must remind myself to pay attention to him because my attention is bouncing around the inside of the foyer. The winding staircase. The chandelier. The artwork. I could spend hours in this room alone studying the beauty captured here. Not to mention the money. One of the paintings is the Rembrandt we studied in my art history class. Stone Operation. Allegory of Touch.

My fascination must be obvious.

He joins me at my observation point a safe distance from a painting worth enough to feed a small country. "What do you think? The painting is quite beautiful, is it not?"

I hesitate then choose discretion. "It's beautiful in what it represents. A renowned artist early in his career, exploring his style. The colors, the detail, the play of light that gives texture and depth. The mere fact that it still exists after four hundred years."

Mr. Romero smiles, a reserved lift of his mouth. He clasps his hands behind his back. "That's a very neutral answer."

It's my turn to laugh. Not only am I used to being Switzerland in the sexuality department, but I'm also an expert at riding the fence in a conversation. As a kid, I was to be seen and not heard. I still live that philosophy. "I've been invited here by someone important to me. I don't want to embarrass her in my first five minutes in the door."

His smile broadens and he drops his clasped hands to his side. "What about the second five minutes you're in the door?"

"All bets are off."

He looks at his watch, then back to the painting.

I wait.

I wait some more.

Finally, he looks at his watch again. "Your second five minutes have begun. What do you think of the painting?"

I rock back on my heels, letting the backpack drop to the floor. Oh boy. "My reaction is more personal than subjective and according to my art appreciation professor, that is an unforgivable flaw." I pause, take a breath. "I admire the artist. He did his own thing despite what others thought of him. I dislike this painting because, unlike the other known works in the series, it's about causing pain. The patient has gone to this person with hope and trust. The act the surgeon-" I air quote the word "-is performing is said to refer to an idiom which means to fool someone. Being made a fool is painful in ways that do not heal easily."

He nods, silent, and I drop my head, sheepish at my outburst. My professor didn't understand my dislike of such a work of art by a grand master. He wasn't a grand master when he painted this, I'd argued. He was a teenager learning the world around him. The world is not always beautiful, even when painted in pretty colors.

"You're very astute, Ms. Fontenot. Most people look at a painting such as this and see only the picture. You look behind for the meaning and as you've pointed out, what you see is not always what you get."

The story of my life.

When I was a child, my aunt and uncle presented a happy family picture for the world. We were neither happy nor a family. Now, I'm finding parts of myself hidden by years of denial and fear. But am I being a fool trusting Lily and Jon with those parts? Are there more things I haven't discovered yet?

The answers whisper easily in my ear, but my heart has a hard time listening.

I look back up to find Mr. Romero studying me as I am studying the painting. I grab my backpack and shoulder it. We talk a bit more about the impressive artwork collection in the foyer. If this is what they have at the entrance, I can't wait to see what's hidden further inside.

TWIST
CHAPTER THREE

We walk through countless hallways and rooms, twisting and turning. I'll never find my way out of this place without going out a window. But the puzzling layout makes me think of another puzzle.

Lily.

When I consider the dinner party at the McMansion and the party at the Masters winery, now this, I wonder how much I really know about her. She either has secret underworld connections or is stinking rich. And if she's rich, why is she sharing a dorm room with the likes of me?

This weekend is supposed to be about trust. Or at least that's my take on the lessons these *ghosts* are supposed to be teaching me. Trust myself. Trust her. Trust Jon. How am I supposed to trust Lily if I don't know who she is?

Mr. Romero opens a door and we walk through, entering a two-story glass atrium. The room is a comfortable ambient temperature but stuffy with the humidity reminiscent of an average summer day. And for good reason. It's floor to ceiling orchids.

If the room could speak it would say *Lily*.

The glass panes are filtered, carefully controlling the amount of light that enters but enough sun shines through that the room is bright. The flowers touch every available surface, hanging pots, elaborate vases on the floor and shelves. And the colors.

Not just the standard red, purple, white and yellow. No. The room is overflowing with blue orchids.

Lily came back to the dorm with a blue orchid one evening, a gift from Jon, but it disappeared the next day. The strain is rare. The ones you find in flower shops are usually dyed. I'm guessing there's no blue dye No. 5 hidden around here.

I know little about horticulture, but I know orchids are flowers that require careful attention. Someone must love these plants - this room - a lot to keep the flowers blooming and in such pristine condition.

"Of all the rooms in the house," Mr. Romero says, interrupting my thoughts. "This is my favorite."

"Why is that?"

"The beauty in this room requires constant attention. It's not something you can ignore. It's a marriage between the caretaker and the flower. There must be a great love for the flower to thrive."

I smile but I feel the cynicism tilting the corners of my mouth. "I've seen the gardens of the house, Mr. Romero. You obviously have exceptionally good gardeners. You don't have to love something to feed and water it." My aunt and uncle proved that point to me long ago.

It's his turn to smile. "Very true, Ms. Fontenot. But weeds and flowers grow differently under the same care when love is applied."

Am I the weed or the flower in this analogy? I was tenacious as a kid, learning to do everything on my own from an early age. From riding my bike to graduating third in my high school class, I received little in the way of support.

And still, I stuck around.

Mr. Romero doesn't wait for my response. In truth, I don't really have one, so I follow him through the atrium and into the outbuilding. He holds open the door and after I pass through, I hear the lock click.

I jerk my head toward the door to see him already pointing to the lock, a hand upraised to stop my protest. He turns the handle and I hear the click again before the door opens once more.

"The door locks from within. You'll be changing clothes and I don't want anyone to walk in uninvited." He locks the door once more, then walks to a small armoire and lays his hand on the exterior. "Inside you'll find an outfit picked out for you. When you've changed, please join me."

He disappears through the pocket door hidden behind the large mirror attached to it, like one of those closet doors from the seventies.

My heart is still pounding like a caged animal, and it takes a few breaths for my vision to escape the tunnel and look around the small room. Other than the armoire and an old-fashioned cushioned settee, the room is bare. No paintings on the walls. No windows.

I try the door, because I have to reassure myself I'm not trapped, and find it opens easily enough. No Harry Potter magic has transformed the atrium outside into anything but the atrium, so I lock the door and go to the armoire.

After the last two evenings my expectations for the clothing I'll be provided are skewed to minimalism. One of the things Lily seems to want to teach me is to be comfortable with my body. It's not that I'm not comfortable with it. Exhibitionism has just never been my thing. Bare skin draws attention. I prefer the camouflage of blue jeans and buttoned up button downs and secret lingerie stashes I keep for myself at night.

But true to form, Lily defies expectation. Hanging in the armoire is a leather dress. I'd seen it in her closet. She wore it to a Mardi Gras party this past season, her picture ending up on the front page of the Times Picayune's entertainment section.

The nip and tuck at the waist are sure to hug every curve. The high neckline will fit like a collar - the only thing missing is a lock - although the high neckline and gauzy bodice is for show only. The plunging decolletage won't leave much to the imagination. The long sleeves are of the same gauzy material, more for show than anything, but leather cuffs secure the material at the wrists.

Did I mention the leather is red? No. Not red.

Crimson.

Like the teddy I wore the night this all started.

Are the collared neckline and cuffs a reminder of my submission to Lily and Jon? A reminder of the rules? Or are they just a fashion choice?

Nothing with Lily is ever as simple as it appears, however.

A pair of matching thigh thigh-high boots wait beneath the dress, the modest heel something I'm grateful for. I pull the dress out of the closet and find a small silk bag dangling from the back of the hanger. Inside, a mask to match the dress and a note.

Even a double headed coin has two faces. Don't be afraid to explore both.

The now familiar 'L' is scrawled across the bottom, but the obscurity of the note is lost on me. When I think of two faces, I think of deceit. My brain jumps back to the painting in the foyer.

What you see is not always what you get.

Jacob. RideShare chauffeur or business student?

Lily. Sexy princess or serious PhD student?

Me. Neutral Switzerland or exotic fantasy land?

Everyone and everything around me seems to have a hidden facet. That's not deceit.

That's humanity.

I dress, keeping my panties and bra since there are no instructions otherwise. If I've learned anything that last two nights, I'll likely be naked soon enough although this outfit doesn't seem in keeping with that theme. It covers more than the previous two outfits combined.

I stash my backpack in the armoire and don my mask, catching site of my reflection when I go to slide open the door. Beneath the edge of the mask, my cheeks are flushed, a dark rosy slash heightened by the color of the leather. There's a jut to my hip as I stand there and for a fleeting second, a surge of power tingles through me. Like electricity over water, it crackles to life and snaps along the nerve endings.

The thigh thigh-high boots kiss the edge of the dress, the thinnest line of pale flesh visible between the two. I was right. The dress finds each curve and valley of my body, the supple leather a duality in softness and support. The collar and cuffs are a subtle reminder of my submission but the boots and dress exude power.

Maybe this is the reference to the coin Lily mentioned in her note: two sides of the same coin. And wasn't it Dominic who told me it was the submissive who had the control in the exchange of power? Lily said the coin had two faces, not two sides. The distinction is small. With a two-sided coin, you expect differences. A double headed coin is identical on both sides. Or is it?

I push aside my questions as I push aside the mirrored door, hiding my reflection and my uncertainty.

Inside, Mr. Romero is waiting. He's removed the suit jacket and tie, the sleeves of his dress shirt rolled up to reveal strong forearms. The two-story room is like most any room in the house I've seen so far. There's beautiful furniture. Exquisite sculpture. Soft light from the second story opaque windows and the overhead chandelier.

But it's the naked woman kneeling at his feet that captures my attention.

TOUCH

CHAPTER FOUR

I close the door behind me, leaning my weight back on my heels as I consider the scene. My mind may not have processed the picture before me, but my pussy is doing a clench and release. The woman's back is to me, her bare bottom resting on her heels. A snug hood covers her head, but that gorgeous ass is achingly familiar.

The surface of every wall on the first floor is covered in mirrored panels. The mirrors give me every angle, every curve of her body. Her skin is flushed, a brushed gold polished to perfection and highlighted by the soft lighting.

Mr. Romero steps between me and the woman, blocking my direct view. "You've given yourself over to Lily this weekend, Gabrielle. Today she wants you to see what it is like to hold the other side of the power in the exchange of domination and submission."

The response that bubbles up is immediate. "But I'm not dominant."

He holds out his hand, gesturing at me from head to toe. "You've hardly uncovered what you are or are not in this world, Gabrielle. Would you have thought yourself capable of submitting to the will of Lily at the start of the weekend? Letting her make the choices you've allowed?"

The things I've given over to Lily the past forty-eight hours shocks me. She's picked my clothes, told me when and where to be, even if I can orgasm.

And I've allowed it.

I'd have laughed in someone's face if they'd suggested such things a few weeks ago. I'd worked ridiculously hard to escape anyone who wanted to control me. Why was I so willing to give it to Lily?

"Then let me rephrase. I don't know how to be a dominant. What if I..." I let my eyes roam the long line of bare flesh from shoulder to hip, the curve of each buttock. "Harm her."

"I'll do my best to make sure that doesn't happen but if something does go wrong," He crosses the room to stand next to me, putting a hand on my shoulder. "Just know that it will be minor, and it will be forgiven."

Putting myself in Lily's hands was one thing. But now Lily is putting herself in my hands.

Trust.

There's that word again. I've trusted Lily so far and she's not let me down. But now the tables are turned. Am I worthy of such trust? I've already broken one rule but last night Dylan and Kylia let me know that mistakes are expected. Mistakes are not unforgivable. I could make them and still be wanted and loved. Mr. Romero is saying the same thing.

Do I believe it?

I realized last night I was done running. I can do this. I will do this.

I nod, not only giving Mr. Romero my consent but giving myself permission.

Mr. Romero and I move to the front of the room and stand before the kneeling woman. Her face is downcast so I can't see anything but the top of her head. I look to her hip, where I expect to find the little kitten tattoos I saw peeking above her jeans that day in the ride share downtown. They're not there. My heart and body tell me this is Lily. However, since I cannot see her face the logical part of my brain is resistant to give her a name.

"Why is she in the hood?"

"It can be difficult to compartmentalize the act of causing pain to cause pleasure, especially with someone you care about. The hood keeps things...neutral."

Neutral. I'm good at neutral.

The woman stands on some unspoken command. I think I might get a look at her eyes - I'd know Lily's eyes anywhere - but no such luck. Only a small, zippered opening is there for the mouth, the lips in a soft line beneath the leather.

Mr. Romero stands at my back, the heat of his body a wall to lean upon. I can look up and see his reflection, but my eyes are all for her.

"Touch her."

My brain begins a cascade of where I should touch her first and my eyes catalog the silky landscape of hills and valleys. Shoulders. Breasts. Belly. Hips. Pubis. I want it all but...

"What if she doesn't want me to touch her somewhere? Or doesn't like how I touch her? What's her safeword?"

"I'm her safeword, Bree. She is yours, given freely and without hesitation." Our eyes meet in the mirror over her shoulder. He nudges my elbow until my arm lifts. My hand is only inches from her body. "Touch her."

The mask ends at the base of her throat, and I see the

long column of her throat work as she swallows. Her mouth remains neutral, neither smiling nor grimacing nor frowning. Just waiting.

I put my finger just beneath the mask, in the small hollow of her throat. Her breathing is slow, measured. I trace a hesitant line to her shoulder, watch the gooseflesh rise in the wake of my touch over her skin. A matching reaction blossoms on my own flesh. I don't pause to wonder why too long.

Next, I move to swell of her breast, heading straight for the nipple. Her mouth opens slightly and a little gasp of breath announces her anticipation. If I've learned one thing from Lily and my weekend so far, it's that anticipation can be its own reward. So I detour.

The first hint of a pout on her mouth tightens those beautiful lips.

A sudden rush of heat excites my body.

I move my attention from the reaction of the body before me - the gooseflesh, the tightening areolas, the pert nipples - to my own. I'm a mirror to the arousal before me. I wish now I'd removed my bra. The leather would feel delightful against my nipples in this state. As it is, the cotton bra only acts as a cushion.

"You like to tease."

It's a statement, not a question from Mr. Romero. I don't take my eyes off *ma cocotte*. The phrase pops into my head just that quickly. Something I remember my father saying to my mother when he would sneak up behind her to steal a kiss. She would jump and playfully swat at him, but she would always turn at the last second and give him a quick peck on the cheek. Her smile lingered long after his arms disappeared from around her body.

"Teasing is its own form of foreplay."

I'd learned this lesson. Lying on the bed, cuffed to the headboard while strong hands explored every hill and valley of my flesh taught me the beauty of the tease.

Mr. Romero holds out a pair of small silver clips. "And not just for the recipient."

He directs me how to apply the nipple clamps, stimulating the soft peaks with flicks and twists until taut, then closing the clamp around the nub slowly. Heat blooms in a blushing wave across *ma cocotte* and she rocks back on her heels from the rush then settles as the sensation ebbs.

A small chain dangles between the breasts and I give it a gentle experimental tug. My reward is a little gasp and a stifled moan.

When her breathing calms, I circle *ma cocotte*, never letting my fingers leave her body. The curve of her hip, the arc of her buttock, the line of her spine as it stretches her lithe body so nicely. I cup the cheek of her ass, letting my hands take the weight of that beautiful body before skimming my fingertips up the obliques and back to her neck.

My fingers read each flex of muscle and wave of goose-flesh as my touch moves along the contour of shoulder back to hip then around the waist to draw her against me.

It's my turn to sigh as her nakedness molds against me and I wish now there was nothing between us. She lifts a hand and curls it around the back of my neck for balance as my first touch dances lightly between her legs. I'm careful though. I can feel the heat. I don't press further into the delicate folds although it's a form of torture for me not to touch her more, deeper.

Her hand covers mine, urging, guiding. I kiss her lightly on the neck and move her hand back to her side. It's my turn, not hers.

We're about the same height. I hadn't realized it before,

always feeling less in her presence. Not because she did anything to make me feel inferior. No, I did that on my own. I always feel less around others. Hiding. Hidden. Invisible.

It was time to turn the tables a little.

Her hand tightens on the nape of my neck, drawing me closer. Her arousal is a heady perfume in the room. I kiss her lightly, just behind the ear, and whisper, "Not yet."

DISCOVERY
CHAPTER FIVE

I t takes every ounce of willpower to untangle her hand from my body and step back from her. But I do it. Because I'm in charge.

At least for the moment.

I look to Mr. Romero. A smile lifts one corner of his mouth and something I can only call pride adds a twinkle to his dark eyes. "You're a natural."

Praise is foreign to me. Sure, I'd received compliments. Pleasant personality. Nice tits. Great paper on the impact of capitalism in communist dictatorships.

But Mr. Romero's words, his ownership of them...they reach me on a level I didn't know still existed. I straighten my spine and square my shoulders. It's out of joy, however. Not out of the need of a lonely little girl to please her elders.

He removes a paddle from a small table behind him and joins me beside *ma cocotte*. A small touch on her shoulder sends her to a tabletop position on the floor without a word from either of them.

"Spanking is a great warm up for any scene. Skin to skin

is an intimate connection between top and bottom. It also allows for access to other pleasure points if desired."

Yeah, I desired other pleasure points.

"It can be taxing on the hands, however."

He goes on to talk about supporting the body and gives me a tutorial on where to spank - the meaty part of buttocks, top of the thighs - and where not to hit - basically anywhere else for now.

He hands over the paddle in his hand, a somewhat flexible device covered in thick, soft leather. It reminds me of a square ping pong paddle, only slightly larger.

I hold the paddle like it's a snake or a broken piece of glass. He expects me to hit *ma cocotte* with this. At least I know this in theory. The practice of it leaves me stunned statue still.

I look up, and for a split second the reflections in the mirrors around the room deceives me. It is Lily holding the paddle, her body shown to perfection in the leather and lace, her attitude a neon sign of confidence and sensuality.

But it's not Lily.

I'm the one holding the paddle. Is this why she left me her outfit? To show me how similar we are behind the mask I wear for the outside world? Maybe I'm not Switzerland. I'm still not Bourbon Street during Mardi Gras, but I'm also no longer Saturday nights with library and laundry.

I raise my hand and land the first smack on *ma cocotte's* beautiful ass. The soft *thwap* of leather on flesh is accompanied by a satisfying blush on her butt cheek. With my free hand, I soothe the red mark, the slight fever of her skin warming my palm.

I raise my hand again and land a few more smacks, always changing the landing location. High on the thigh. Middle of the cheek. Thigh. Cheek. Left. Right. Left Right.

After every smack I stop and soothe the ever-reddening skin. *Ma cocotte's* head remains down, her face hidden from me by more than the mask.

"Don't be afraid, Gabrielle."

I'd almost forgotten he is in the room. I look up.

"It's ok to take what is being offered to you."

The weight of his words pulls in meaning from the rest of my life. Never has anyone offered me something without setting a price to be paid first. You can have dinner if... You can attend graduation if... I'll love you if...

Ma cocotte wiggles her ass in invitation and it's all I need.

I add a little more weight with the next few cracks of the paddle, her ass blossoming nicely in varying shades of rosy pink. On the tenth or so strike, *ma cocotte's* head lifts and I see her mouth open, tongue darting out to moisten her bottom lip. She widens her legs, lifting her ass even higher.

I lose count but keep my focus. My goal is singular. Bring her pleasure. I can smell her arousal, see the effect on her body. Her bottom lip is tucked between her teeth. Her toes are curled against the padded mat.

What is happening between my legs is a tidal wave of heat and desire. If I'm not careful, I'll orgasm without ever touching myself.

Her breathing is slowing so I lower the paddle and kneel by her hip. I caress her reddened backside. "Breathe, *ma cocotte*."

Her shoulders rise and fall. I lightly stroke the outer lips of her very wet pussy. When I press one finger into her channel, her breath studders.

I lean over her shoulder and whisper into her ear. "Your pussy is so wet." I ease another finger inside of her. She pushes against my hand. "Do you know how wet it makes me knowing I can do that to you?" I find her clit while pumping my fingers in and out of her. "That you'll let me do that to you? I've never known such--" I have to stop because the words clog in my chest before even making it to my tongue. She must sense my emotion because she nuzzles my cheek and even though I can't see her face I feel her heart next to mine.

"Do you want to come, *ma cocotte*?"

A new wash of heat coats my fingers.

"Yes." The word is soft, throaty.

"Will you come without my permission?"

She rides my hand, my fingers, desperate little gasps and moans rushing past my ear. "No."

Power. It's a pure aphrodisiac. I see why people want it, search for it, wield it with such ease to get what they want. But it's only half the fun.

I circle her clit some more, the nub swollen and sopping wet. With my free hand, I find the clamps on her nipples and release the first, shushing her as her shoulders tense as the sensation hits her body. "Are you ready?"

She nods, beyond words as her hips pump against my hand. Her body tightens around my fingers, rapid little quakes already hinting at the impending release.

I release the final clamp. "Then come for me."

Her body jerks with the orgasm as it ripples through her body, clenching from her pussy to toes, then back up to her shoulders and down to her pussy once more.

As her body relaxes, I ease her to her side and spoon her from behind. She curls her hands around mine and draws it beneath her chin. We are a cocoon of sated lust. I may not have orgasmed with her, but my body is content against her.

OZ

CHAPTER SIX

The ride back to campus is silent. Whether Jacob knows what happened or not, he senses my need for quiet and puts me in the back of the car, a bottle of water and a can of chilled Cheerwine at my disposal.

I consume both as I unsuccessfully avoid overthinking my feelings.

I'm falling for Lily.

I know logically it doesn't make sense. Our relationship was a surface one until a week ago but my heart, too long ignored in my life, has roared to life.

I love her.

And she loves Jon.

She said our first night she and Jon wanted someone they could share. Did I want to be an add-on in their relationship?

I'm not certain my feelings for Jon. I care for him. I like him. But Lily...she is the moon, the sun, the gravity holding me on the earth.

Will I take half of her heart if I can't have it all? More importantly, is Jon truly willing to share?

Shortly after I arrived to live with my aunt and uncle, I'd overheard my aunt say to a friend that a bicycle didn't need a third wheel.

Back in the room, I curl up on Lily's bed, creating a nest of her pillows around me. If I can't hold her, at least I can breathe in the scent of her.

When I wake, there is another package on the bed. The note simply gives a time. Lily is confident I know what to do by now. This dress...this one almost makes me cry uncle as I hold it up with two fingers and look at myself in the mirror. It's a complete one-eighty from last night's fleece track suit. But it's the last night. The final ghost.

I have nothing to lose at this point.

I dress and wait for my ride, working hard to keep my thoughts from falling down a rabbit hole. If this is the end, there will be time for tears and regrets later.

The ride to our destination is brief. When the car stops against the curb, Jacob escorts me from the limo. The sign overhead marks the building as "The Velvet Cage." My heart does a little two-step. Even on a Sunday night, the crowd is waiting three deep outside.

I've heard of the club around campus – the place to be, the most *in place* among the *in crowd*. Other rumors circulate about the club – secret rooms, secret pleasures for the right price. Nothing illegal.

Just illicit.

I'm not exactly part of the *in crowd* and haven't been to the club since starting school. Looks like that is about to change. The crowd gathered parts and stares and I unconsciously clutch Jacob's arm a little tighter. He pats my hand and smiles down at me.

He leans over and whispers against my ear, "You belong. Don't doubt that."

He slides his gaze over my dress, a sapphire blue number I'd nearly refused to put on tonight. Unlike the first dress, whose hem barely protected my ass, this dress drops below my knees. Not that it matters. Calling it material is an ironic play on words, there in name only. It's completely sheer. The lacy mesh cheeky panty covers the important bits on the bottom. Still...it's not much.

"That dress." He whistles under his breath. "That dress is probably illegal in the daylight."

Chills dance around my body at his words. I may not always believe a compliment, but I'm not immune to them. Looking at the crowd as we walk forward, however, I see open lust on the men's faces and undisguised hatred on the women's faces. Tonight, I'm a believer.

The two men guarding the entrance nod to Jacob and open the first set of double doors. The crowd gasps and shouts their indignity at having to wait while I'm ushered inside. I sympathize. I'm also secretly pleased with the special treatment.

I've always stood on the edge, wanting to be pulled inside but never getting the invite. Today I belong, and it does more than put a kick to my step as we pass through the first set of massive glass doors separating the world outside from the one inside.

It puts my ego and id on a pedestal.

It feels good to be the chosen, but there's still a vacancy at my side I want filled. Two faces immediately come to mind and the fierceness with which my heart contracts would frighten me any other time.

I want them. I'm not sure how I fit into their lives yet. Am I a plaything to amuse them for a bit before being cast aside? The desired toy on Christmas Day forgotten within a month. Or is it more than that?

I want it to be more than that and the admission scares me to the very core of my heart and soul. Logic says it's too soon. My heart tells me I am wasting time because the decision has been made and I am just keeping myself from the happiness at hand by being stubborn.

But it's more than stubbornness. Experience has taught me long ago *wanting* did not mean *getting*. It usually means losing more than I originally wanted.

We're standing in a small foyer area now. A coat check clerk stands ready to dispense a randomly generated code to a bank of lockers. I stash my purse. Since I don't wear a lot of make-up, I don't have the need to refresh it throughout the night. It's good to be low maintenance at times.

Jacob guides me to the next set of doors where the most stunningly beautiful person I have ever seen is watching me cross the space between us. It takes me a moment, but I recognize the emcee from the winery. They are less flamboyant but still own the space around them.

The well-tailored suit hugs the lines of their body in all the right places. The color – a deep burgundy – might look garish on some but it brings out the bronze in their skin tone and the auburn and gold in the lush waves of hair trailing down their back.

Long slender fingers reach out for mine and lift my hand to their mouth. A soft kiss across the knuckles.

A seductive smile tilts up one side of their mouth. "Good evening, Gabrielle. Welcome to The Velvet Cage."

They roll a stamp across the back of my hand leaving the imprint of a bird's cage. The image of a sparrow is escaping the opened cage door.

The fact they know me or expect my arrival doesn't surprise or scare me. Progress?

"Is that the club's usual stamp or am I special?"

"You're definitely special, Gabrielle." My name rolls across the luxurious tenor of their voice. "But this is our brand. Freedom for those who seek it. Freedom from any restrictions found in everyday life for everyday people." Their eyes find Jacob over my shoulder and a hint of mischievousness sparks. They execute a half-bow, tipping the toe of their four-inch platforms behind the opposite ankle. "Hi Jacob."

"Hi River. Lookin' hot tonight."

"Don't I always?" The tip of their tongue darts out to touch the peak of the top lip. Sobering, River snaps a sharp salute toward the two men. "Your charge is safely delivered in my hands, Sir Gatekeeper. I shall guard her with my life."

Jacob leans over and pecks a chaste kiss on the corner of River's mouth. "Thanks, love." He does the same to me. "Gabrielle, I'll see you later. Enjoy your evening."

We watch Jacob walk from the foyer because it can't be helped. You have to watch a man that gorgeous walk away.

"Damn."

"Ain't it the truth."

River extends an arm and I tuck my hand in the crook.

"We're off to see the wizard," River exclaims, and leads me into Oz.

FLIGHT
CHAPTER SEVEN

A haze swirls around the dimly lit interior, an undulating curtain illuminated by the flashing lights. River guides me through the crowd and despite the press of bodies at the bar, an empty stool waits at the end. They lift me effortlessly onto the seat. They don't stand much taller than me but there's strength behind the grip that circles my waist.

I cross my legs and wish I had my clutch in my lap. It would give me something to do with my hands. Instead, I take River's hand before they can pull fully away from me. They're about to leave me alone...to what end?

They brush the hair from my face and press their cheek to mine. "I'll be around if you need me. You have your safe-word." Face to face again, they cup my face between those long fingers, holding it gently but securely so I can't look away. "Tonight, focus on freeing yourself from the cage."

A quick squeeze of my hand then they disappear into the hive of people rather than back toward the front doors.

I watch the crowd, searching the faces for some hint of recognition, for Lily or Jon, Dylan, Jacob, even one of the fab foursome would be welcome at this point. But I see noth-ing. I turn my barstool back to face the bar, and instead find I'm face to face with myself.

The back wall of the bar is a placement of hexagonal mirrors, but each must be tilted minutely because the images are all slightly different. The lights play off the beveled edges but it's seeing myself in a multitude of images that really captures me. So many different angles of the same person.

I am not a social person by nature, preferring intimate gatherings to the craze of flesh-pressing in a club. My courage begins to sag. *This is a terrible mistake*, I tell myself. *I should leave*. I search harder for Jacob, scanning the bodies writhing on the dance floor.

If I can get the bartender's attention I can ask if they know Lily. Or maybe I can manage to find River in the club. I slide off the stool, no concrete plan in mind but needing to move.

Then I see him.

My knight from the winery.

Marcus.

He watches me from the edge of crowd and his rapt attention stills my movements. I look to my left and right to see if his gaze is for another but there's no one close enough.

Marcus nods and the bartender breaks away from the throngs waiting. He pops a single serving bottle of cham-pagne, pours the bubbly liquid into a flute then slides the glass toward me.

"I didn't order anything."

He points to Marcus on the dance floor. "With the compliments of the house, miss."

I perch back on the stool and cradle the glass in my

hand then lift it in salute, wondering if he was sent by Jon and Lily or if his ownership of the bar is a coincidence.

Doubtful. The weekend has been too well planned for anything to be a coincidence. I look at the label on the champagne. Sure enough. Masters Winery.

I taste the gold liquid, the heady flavor smooth and rich. The warmth tickles its way through my system. A few more sips. My desire to leave dissipates on the courage of bubbly champagne. The music coils around my senses, easing the tension from my limbs.

I motion with my now empty glass to the bartender.

"Sorry," he smiles, but it isn't sorrow I see lifting the corners of his mouth. He takes the glass from my hands and nods toward Marcus across the room. "You only get one."

One glass, like the other night at dinner. That can't be a coincidence. At least it was real champagne and not cider this time.

I return my attention to the mysterious gentleman who wants to soften me but not ply me with alcohol. I still can't tell his age, and the strobing lights in the darkness don't help. But I was up close and personal with him last night and the only thing crystal clear regardless of the lighting is the man radiates power.

He's dancing provocatively with his partner, their bodies swaying in unison. Her breasts rub his chest, her thighs cradle his like they'd melted around the limb. Everything about their bodies, their movements, their unspoken language of the dance speaks of sex.

His body may have been hers at the moment, but his eyes were only for me. The walls of my pussy contract and the warmth in my body centers in one glorious spot.

River's words come to mind.

Freedom from restrictions found in everyday life for everyday people.

I slip from the stool again and look down to make sure my feet are on the floor.

On some hidden cue, the female dancer glides away to join another couple, their movements never ceasing as she moves into their space. The three embrace, kiss, dance.

A slow roll of jealousy leaves me cold and hot at the same time. I'm ready to be back with Jon and Lily. Face to face. No more hiding behinds masks and darkness. But Lily said this weekend is supposed to be about my education. What am I learning? Stubbornness silences the voice inside my head that talks about trust and freedom from inhibitions.

Marcus is standing alone on the dance floor but not for long. Another woman approaches but he shakes his head without giving her a side glance. He leaves the dance floor without a look back and eats up the space between us in long, slow steps.

The abandoned woman's gaze drill into his back as he weaves through the crowd toward me, jealousy and anger narrowing her eyes to thin slits. Victory surges through me. I'm not the type to inspire jealousy in women. But I can see the addictive nature of the drug in being the chosen one.

Marcus wears only black - a running theme among the people connected to Lily. It's not a tuxedo but the effect is no less stunning. Tailored flat front trousers cup him intimately and leave nothing to the imagination. The Italian jacket gives him a professional look but does not mark him as someone stilted by board rooms or electronic calendars.

Beneath, a plain t-shirt molds to his broad, muscled chest. The familiar Austin alligator boots are a stark contrast to the high-end clothing and hint at the bad boy reflected in the possessive gaze.

When my eyes finally return to his face, I realize he's doing his own assessment. What does he see? The heat of his perusal stalks up my legs, skim over my calves, then up to my hips and thighs. The hooded eyes linger on my breasts. I wonder if my nipples are visible in the dim light, and they pucker and harden at the possibility. When his gaze reaches my eyes he smiles...no, it isn't a smile. It's a smirk. A shiver courses down my spine.

"Good evening." His voice is a sultry rumble, the eastern European weight to his words less pronounced tonight. Regardless, I'm picturing him stalking through dark corridors at midnight, a hapless virgin tossed casually over his shoulder. She's not fighting much, though.

I pull myself from the wayward thoughts. "Good evening," I finally manage.

"We didn't really meet last night. I'm Marcus Keyes."

Keyes.

It's too much of a coincidence. I decide against asking. I'll let the night unfold. Tonight is about freedom.

And there's always Rule #1.

I'm surrounded by people. I don't have to go anywhere; do anything I don't want. Even if I can't find River or Jacob, there's always RideShare.

I relax into the decision, breathing easier, the tension plucked away.

Marcus takes my hand and I notice a black leather band braided around his wrist – a key dangling from its length. There's a surge of...victory perhaps...at making the right call.

He lifts my hand to his mouth, his lips lingering a moment longer than necessary against my knuckles. The brush of his mouth ignites a fiery flash which ribbons through my body, curling around my insides like hot chocolate on a winter's eve.

"Welcome to my place, Gabrielle." The use of my name doesn't surprise me. He caresses my palm with the pad of his thumb, a decidedly intimate gesture if my reaction is any indication. Heat and arousal and dirty thoughts head on a collision path for my pussy.

Before I can think of a response, he pulls me against his body and murmurs, "Dance with me."

I shake my head. Talk, yes. Dance?

"I don't dance," I say aloud but inside I'm begging for him to make me dance. I have memories, few and hazy, of dancing and feeling safe. Before everything went to shit in my life.

Our bodies hover less than an inch apart as he leans forward and a mixture of sandalwood and pine assault my senses. He presses a hand to the small of my back, his fingers brushing the curve of my buttocks. The possessiveness reflected in his eyes transmits to my body and I knew he would win in any situation he chose.

Marcus whispers again in my ear, his lips brushing the lobe. "Dance with me, Bree."

His voice, sultry, throaty, skims along the raw ends of my nerves. I start to protest again but instead let him lead me onto the dance floor. He moves us through the crowd to the center of the floor, my hand a captive in his.

When he stops, he turns and wraps his left arm tightly around my waist, pulling me into the arc of his body. The swell of his cock brushes my belly and my sex flutters. Our joined hands curl between us, his knuckles brushing the peaks of my hard nipples.

Before Jon and Lily, I'd never had such a visceral reaction to another human being. Even with the others I'd met through this experience – Dominick, Kenneth, Kylie, Vivian, Jacob – the attraction was shaded with curiosity and caution.

Marcus scares me because I knew I'd follow him anywhere. Do anything he asked. Instead of responding with fear, as expected, however, a calmness settles over me.

OFFERING
CHAPTER EIGHT

I relax as our bodies move to the music. Marcus guides me skillfully and his lead is easy to follow. Each move translates through his muscled limbs to my smaller ones. He leans his head down to mine and presses his cheek to my face. I close my eyes, lulled by the rush of his breath against my ear, his fingers intertwined with mine.

With the next song, he holds me tighter, my breasts crushed against his thick chest. His knee parts my thighs and my dress hitches up a bit. Instead of feeling self-conscious about my state of dress (or undress) I feel strangely sexual, bold and wanton. Besides, he's seen me in less.

I press the flat of my hands to Marcus' abdomen and slowly slide then up and around his neck. Both of his hands circle around my waist to rest on the swell of my buttocks. He's close enough to feel his erection harden against the plane of my belly.

His grip is firm, controlling. Where he moves, I follow. Where he touches, I burn.

We dance for what seems like hours and the current

sizzling between us electrifies the air. When we tire, we escape the human wall of undulating flesh, to a private booth in a corner of the dance floor, somehow immune to the noise and press of bodies.

He calls it the champagne bubble.

He's sitting close enough it's not necessary to raise our voices. His words carry enough weight on their own.

"Later tonight I will ask for your submission, Gabrielle. I will be responsible for you this evening, along with Lily and Jon. This is a role I take very seriously. First, I want to know you, yes? As you Americans say, just between us."

And we talk.

Talk of everything, anything. Well, anything except himself. He avoids direct questions about his past. I try to do the same, but he draws out the answers and it feels safe telling him what he wants to know.

I've not told many of my situation with my aunt and uncle. Jon and Lily know the high points. Marcus provides a safe repository. He'll be gone after tonight, after all. What harm is there in sharing that part of myself with him?

Back on the dance floor, few words pass between us. Our bodies do the communicating. The combination of Marcus' commanding presence and the music and my own building anticipation work on my senses until my thoughts and vision blur and become a spiral of desire and demand for release. I let the music move my body as it wants. I have neither the desire nor the will to resist.

It. Is. Amazing.

As the music fades one last time, Marcus does not release me. Instead, he tightens his embrace and draws me upward. Our lips hover, his breath mingling with mine. I want him to kiss me. I want more than that. But I'll settle for a kiss right now.

His tongue snakes out and flicks the bow of my lip. "Will you submit to me tonight, Gabrielle?"

The realization of why we are together comes rushing back and my head spins even faster. Thoughts buzz around my brain and realization dawns through the fog, hazy, distant.

The key.

Marcus will teach me something this night. This night, only. I tamp down the pang of disappointment before it has a chance to do much more than spark. Tonight is about freedom. I'm the boring swallow breaking free of her cage. Is he to be a one-night stand to free me of my inhibitions? Or, like the ghost of Christmas Past, is he to show me what I have and where I went wrong and free me from the regret I harbor?

Whatever he is teaching, I want to learn.

"Yes."

"Let's go upstairs."

TAKEN
CHAPTER NINE

We move through the crowd before my thoughts find a coherent path, my hand wrapped securely in his. The key he wears bumps the inside of my wrist and the silver dangling from my neck kisses the curve of my breasts.

Marcus opens a door to reveal a staircase and motions me inside. As I take the first step, the door closes a second later, putting us alone in the dimly lit corridor. I stop and choke down the rush of panic. Everyone so far has shown me I'm not trapped. Dominick with the cuffs on the bed. Mr. Romero with the locked door to the atrium. The only thing holding me prisoner so far is my own fear and distrust.

"When you're ready, Gabrielle."

Marcus has made no move to touch me. He waits patiently. I study his face and the earlier attraction pushes aside the fear, buoyed by my feelings for Lily and Jon. I turn and take the stairs, his heavy footfalls behind me comforting.

Marcus' hands slide up the back of my thighs, lifting my dress to cup my nearly bare buttocks in his palms.

My heart pounds furiously, each beat vibrating in the tender flesh between my legs. Heat radiates through my belly, my breasts pucker as the warmth rolls through me, my sex awash in liquid fire.

I stop at the top, my left leg one step up from my right. Even with the added height of the stairs, he is taller than me. A soft moan escapes as he gently squeezes each cheek.

"Such a beautiful ass." He brushes his lips across my neck and I shudder. "Sweet." His finger breaches the cleft between my buttocks and slides down to tease the outer ridge of my femininity. I gasp and clutch the railing for support. Already lightheaded from the desire, I shut my eyes to the lights dancing before my vision.

Marcus gives my left cheek a playful slap and I let out an uncool *eep* in surprise.

He growls against the hollow of my back. "Upstairs. Now."

As we near the door I notice the special lock beneath the knob – three key holes. The top slot is already taken. Lily and Jon. Marcus removes the key on his wrist and places it in the middle slot. He turns to me, tracing a path with his hands from my erect nipples to the valley where the single key dangles.

My breathing slows. Every nerve in my body goes on instant alert. The moment of truth waits behind this door. Am I brave enough to be the adventurous woman I want to be? Lily and Jon trust that I am, otherwise they wouldn't have gone to all this trouble. They promised I would be safe.

I must trust them.

I must trust in myself if I wanted the freedom this night was going to provide.

Besides, I have built in safeguards: the safeword and Jacob.

Like last night, moving forward is a choice. My choice. I had to give Dominick a key. Tonight, it takes three keys. One will not work without the others, like a relationship. Each must cooperate, work together.

I withdraw the chain and hand it to Marcus. He takes the final key and inserts it into the bottom slot. As sexually charged as the moment is, I can't help but read some subtle message into the position of the keys. The top – Lily and Jon – is clear. The bottom – me – is clear. What does Marcus' place in the middle mean exactly?

My thoughts are interrupted as the door clicks open. Marcus turns the knob but keeps it closed. He pivots, our bodies close enough I can smell the champagne on his breath, see the tiny lines fan out from the corner of his eyes.

"I want you to know this has nothing to do with tonight. If I'd met you any other time and we'd shared tonight, I'd do the same thing."

Before I can ask what that means he circles his right hand around the nape of my neck, drawing me toward him. "I'm going to kiss the hell out of you, Gabrielle. Say no if you want me to stop."

He waits several beats, our eyes play tag with one another then his lips crush mine in a demanding, melt-my-panties kind of kiss.

If I had any breath I'd gasp or squeak or something, but I'm lost as he digs his hands into the hair on each side of my head, tunneling his fingers around my scalp. He tilts my head to give him a better angle and deepens the kiss if he could get deeper than the molten core of my soul.

I wrap my fingers in the lapel of his jacket, wanting him closer, already regretting that we'll only have this night. No, not regret. I'll savor it. Use it to start my new life.

His tongue explores my mouth. I shudder at the intensity in his touch and pour it back on him. It is everything I expect. He releases me and I fall back an inch, breathless.

Something dark and primitive smolders in his eyes. "I shouldn't have done that."

I lift a hand and touch the wetness of our kiss on his mouth, bring a fingertip to my lips and lick away the moisture. "I disagree."

A deep breath fills his chest, held for a long moment before he lets it out deliberately. In control once again. "You are quite unexpected, Gabrielle."

I surprised myself to be honest.

Words remain unspoken on his tongue. I can read that in his eyes despite the shadows obscuring his face. He closes his eyes against my exploration, and swallows hard before speaking again.

"Do you trust Lily and Jon?"

I hesitate because I always hesitate when it came to trust. But my heart answers for me. "Yes." *I want to.*

He turns away without waiting for me to respond and disappears into the dark room without a word. I follow more slowly, waiting on a light to click on. Nothing.

"Marcus?" I call out, hearing the unease waver on my tongue.

No reply.

I call his name again but still receive no answer. My unease slips closer to panic. I don't know how big the room we entered is. It could be the size of the dance floor downstairs, leaving plenty of space for Lily and Jon to hang on the periphery. Or it could be the size of a closet.

There's movement to my right and I snap my head toward the sound. My pulse throbs in my throat. Something brushes my arm and I step back but hit an object that could only be a male body. I'm seized from both sides as four meaty hands clamp down on my arms.

RETREAT
CHAPTER TEN

I struggle against the vice-like grip of my captors. "Marcus." Panic wells up inside but I push it down more easily this time.

"Silence." The voice echoes in the darkness coming from every corner of the room. Definitely not a room the size of a closet.

The sound of Marcus' voice, tight with power, intimately soft, stills my movements. I'm not released, however. The two bodies I can feel around me but not see shift positions and one pair of hands now hold me.

Something flutters against my cheek then covers my eyes. I'm being blindfolded again. What is it with the blindfolds? My captors release me, and I immediately lift my hands to remove the blindfold but Marcus' voice stops me.

"Don't." The tone borders on harsh. I pause.

"We write our stories based too much on what we see, Gabrielle. Who we are is defined by material things – our looks, our clothes. White for innocence, red for seductress. But who we are comes from much deeper." A hand skims across my breast, my shoulder, my hip.

Air drags past the lump in my throat with each breath. Pinpricks of fear dimple and chill my flesh.

A light hums to life overhead. I look toward the sound. Unlike the other nights when I was blindfolded with a gauzy material that allowed some hint of what was going on around me, no light penetrates the heavy mask covering my eyes.

Without the light, my attention is forced beyond the visual. The feel of the carpet beneath my toes. The weight of Marcus' hands on my flesh.

The smell of Lily's perfume – orchids and fresh linen.

"Without the clutter of the material world you truly get to know yourself."

The words echo inside of me as sharply as they bounce against the walls of the room that holds me.

I've always let what others think shape my perception of myself. My aunt and uncle saw me as a nuisance, so I thought of myself as a burden. A one-time lover branded me a disappointment, so I became Switzerland. Lily and Jon, on the other hand, see me through different eyes.

But I fight their vision.

Why can't I see myself that way as well?

"Undress for me." Again, that tone brooks no disobedience.

The rational side of my brain goes into overdrive. I know Marcus is in the room. At least two others, probably male, are with him. Hopefully Lily and Jon stand at the ready. But who else is here?

Last night I had the security of knowing the faces of my *ghosts*. Except for Marcus, I don't know who is out there. What are they thinking? What do they see? A risk taker who gave her submission to a total stranger? A boring, nearly virginal coed who'll go to any lengths after one night of hot sex with the man and woman of her dreams? A scared girl in over her head?

Check, check, and check.

Lily's name hovers at the back of my throat. Fuck. I hope they are close.

"Do you want to leave?" Sarcasm drips from Marcus' words, salt in the wound. Where is my sultry European god of an hour ago? "Quit. Go home to your safe Saturday nights?"

The rush of adrenaline swerves to humiliation then anger as Marcus so easily reads my retreat.

"I'm not sure this is what I had in mind when I agreed to submit."

"What did you have in mind, Gabrielle?"

His voice circles me but I can't get a real sense of where he stands. I try to follow his movements with my head but they change to quickly.

He takes my right hand, trailing his fingers up my arm. "Do you find what you need at night, when you are alone? Is your dream lover enough? I think you require a real touch. A strong touch."

My face flames and I jerk my arm away but the sensation of his touch remains. I clasp my hands in front of my body, my thumbs battling a game of thumb war with each other as my nervousness plays itself out.

"Who will you trust tonight, Gabrielle?"

Lily said all my lessons would be about trust. I've put myself fully in their hands, letting them do things I'd never considered before.

Isn't that trust?

Then my thumb rests on the top of my hand where River stamped the bird cage. I know it is a trick of my mind, but I can feel the ink on my skin, its mark, its meaning.

I think of the open door, the little sparrow flying free. Isn't that what I want? I want to be free. But free of what? I am on my own. Alone. You don't get more freedom than that. No one to question my choices. No one to answer to. No one to care.

"If you will not trust yourself to experience the passion of life, you will never be truly free."

Was he right? My freedom had created a nice little cage where I lived. Door closed to the world.

No, I didn't need freedom *from* anything except myself.

Is that the lesson? It's not about trusting Lily and Jon.

It's about trusting myself.

My aunt and uncle didn't just steal my childhood with their little games and unloving hearts. It wasn't about what they wouldn't provide for me.

It was that I kept looking to them to provide it. I'd picked the wrong people to love and depend on back then. I'd not allowed myself to make the same mistake since then.

My anger turns sharply to something more dangerous: determination. I stiffen my arms at my sides, fists tightly clenched. I slow my breathing. I'd learned to deal with control freaks from my aunt and uncle. I can handle this.

"That's better." Again, the voice moves, slides around me, circles me, folds me into its warmth. "Now, undress for me."

I crook my right hand behind my neck and find the zipper, drawing it downward to meet with the fingers of my other hand. As the material slides past my shoulders, I resist the urge to grab the dress and turn and run.

Deep breaths, I remind myself as the dress slips past my hips to pool at my feet. A hand grazes my calf, then lifts my right foot to remove my shoe. The left shoe follows. My nipples harden and the flesh around them puckers at the cool air. Then, quite to my surprise, my sex quivers.

"You will learn that giving up control can be pleasurable."

I manage to bite back the *never* that almost makes it to my lips. I'm not an idiot. He might control my actions but I soften the blow with the memory of Lily. The memory of the previous nights in her care. I am in charge. No one will make me beg ever again.

Then I think of last night, of hovering on the brink of orgasm until given permission to tip over the edge to release.

At least not unless I want to.

As if reading my thoughts, Marcus asks, "Do you remember Sir Dominick's rule?"

My cheeks burn. So do other places. No orgasms without permission. "Yes."

"And your rule from last night?"

Kneel before my dominant. I hate that rule. I really, really do. "Yes."

"Good. Tonight, you are not permitted to speak except to say *yes, master* or *no, master*."

My stomach does a little flip. I open my mouth to speak but hesitate.

"You may ask your question."

"What about my safeword?"

"The rule for tonight, Gabrielle. You have no safeword. I will decide when you've had enough."

A tightness coils in my chest and my spine goes ramrod straight. It's all or nothing.

"Do you understand?"

I hear Kenneth's words in my head in reference to his

pet, Kylia. *We would never break the faith of those who give us their submission.*

The desire of the dominant is the happiness and safety of the submissive. Vivienne's words the night of the party at the winery were sincere.

Everything so far has proven Lily to be a person I can trust. I am no longer a child at the mercy of others who will betray me. "I understand."

A sound comes at me from the darkness but before I can react a sharp sting bites my buttock. I jump but the hands holding me tighten and prevent me from moving much. "What the fuck?"

This time I hear the whip slice the air before the stinging crack catches me mid-thigh, a thousand fingers of disapproval biting my flesh. "Dammit, Marcus—"

A third lash wraps around my knees. I bite back the oath dancing on my tongue.

Okay, I think. Maybe retreat is the better part of valor.

REBELLION
CHAPTER ELEVEN

I purse my lips tightly. The three lashes are heat lightening against my skin, painful enough to make me acutely aware of the blood coursing through my body. The pulse deep in my sex has never been stronger.

I don't know which surprises me more: allowing someone to do this to me or actually being aroused by the process.

"Do you understand?"

He expects me to resist then retreat. Perhaps Lily and Jon do as well and that is why they kept this *lesson* for last. Show me the pleasure first, then the pain. This is truly about limits tonight. Without trust there is no submission. Without submission...can I find freedom by giving in to another?

The memory of my night with them quickens my heartbeat. I think of Lily. Jon. I want more nights in their arms, our bodies curled tightly against one another.

But for that to happen, I have to trust them completely.

Resolve steels my spine. "Yes...master."

I swear I hear a grin of satisfaction when he says, "And yet you are still standing."

The voice is behind me now. His fingers on the back of my neck – rough, impersonal – pressing downward until I bend at the knees and sink slowly to the floor.

Rebellion is a tangible force in my chest, on my tongue. My skin tingles with the need to release every bit of it upon him. I lean forward, my forehead against my hands, my ass riding high as my pride sinks to the tile.

I slow my breathing but the blood is white hot beneath my skin.

"Prepare her."

My eyes snap open beneath the mask but before I can move both wrists are captured and manacled in a soft leather binding. I stand with assistance and pull at the restraints as my arms are drawn over my head. Metal clanks. Memories collide. My heart thuds in my chest. I search for the cuff release but don't find it.

A deeper arousal ribbons through me, deeper than fear, stronger than anger. "No, Marcus. Not this."

Two more slices through the air – snap, snap – and my ass is on fire. I cry out but bite my tongue against the curses.

"You are not a coward, Gabrielle." Marcus' voice whispers in my ear. "Is this what you fear most? Being trapped? Thinking you have no escape?"

Would he respect my safeword if I used it? Do I want to use it? Do I want to tap out of the final test?

His hand snakes around from behind to cup my right breast. He rolls the nipple between his thumb and forefinger and the nub jumps to life at his expert touch. I curse my traitorous flesh.

Is he tempting me to retreat? Or daring me to stay? Each

beat of my heart pounds in the tight spaces between my legs.

I force back the memories crowding at the front of my brain. Memories of darkness and confinement, the frantic search for freedom, comforting arms.

Those flashes of fear are now mixed with desire and need. Lily and Jon have tested each fear. Fear of being trapped. Fear of making the wrong decision. Fear of making a mistake.

All these things I'd confessed to Marcus just hours earlier.

Each ghost Lily has chosen has shown me I am safe. But do I believe it? Will Marcus use them all against me?

"You treasure your freedom, don't you, Bree?"

Apparently, he will. My carefully constructed walls begin to rebuild, brick by brick.

Freedom is the only thing in life I can call my own. "Yes, master."

The response comes automatically but sounds alien to my ears, my voice fading beneath the roar of betrayal. I'm such a fool. Again.

"But you desire to be controlled, as well." He moves his hand from the left nipple to the right. "It is...safer."

Marcus abandons the nipple and I groan inwardly at the sudden absence but his hand does not withdraw. I hate my weakness. Hate myself for still wanting what he offers. How do I hate being trapped but crave being controlled like this?

"Do you want to give me control of your body, Bree?"

His fingers trail over the still burning cheeks of my ass where the whip kissed my flesh, curving around to the plane of my belly, easing lower until they caress the bared flesh of my pussy. His fingers tease and taunt, warm and electric, and the folds of my sex quiver in anticipation.

"Do you?"

Two answers are allowed. Yes and no. Is my answer really no? I have total control of my life now. Has that made me happy? Content? If I give myself over, can I find these things?

Breathless, I say, "Yes, master."

I want my life to be my own but not on my own. I didn't want someone controlling my every thought or action. I want what I'd found this weekend – teachers, lovers, friends. People to fill the empty places in my being. Someone to show me more of what I'd glimpsed with Jon and Lily.

Two fingers part the tender folds of my sex and I arch up on the restraints, not to pull away but to give him better access. His touch sizzles in the wash of my arousal.

"Is this what you want, sweet Bree?" He dips one finger into the pool of juices bathing the inner walls of my canal, pressing into the tight sheath, a welcome intrusion. When he withdraws, I let my body follow his movements, wanting to keep the sensation as long as possible.

"You didn't answer me." *Crack*! The sting whips around my waist to hug my hip. The pain...oh the sweet, awful pain...I feel the liquid heat of my sex coat the inside of my thighs.

"Control is a double-sided coin. By *giving* me control, you are the one in ultimate control?"

His voice fades a bit as if he is walking away but the thick carpeting absorbs his footsteps.

Is he right? Do I maintain control by giving it away? I choose who. I choose when. I even choose how much control to give them with my safeword, the ability to stop everything, without question, a simple word away.

Marcus as the dominant is in charge. But I, as the submissive, am in total control.

"Yes, master."

FREEDOM
CHAPTER TWELVE

I hear the rustle of cloth and wonder what Marcus will do next. My body tingles in anticipation, my emotions suddenly as light and bright as they'd ever been. What happened before with my life is not happening now.

Then I truly had no control. Now, today, with Lily and Jon, I have it all. They've shown me that I am the one in charge of my life after all. Not anything or anyone else. I think my heart will burst from my chest with gratitude. With love for these two people.

There's a presence – different than Marcus. A different electricity hums through the air.

I step forward but the chains restrict my range of motion and clank angrily overhead when I test their limits. The presence disappears quickly. I lower my head and again sense the nearness, but if it is there they avoid coming too close this time.

As silently as they appear, the unseen presence fades.

I wonder if my imagination is working overtime like the night with Dominick or if Marcus and I are alone or if others are watching this scene unfold like at last night's festivities.

Jacob promised to be close and a blush of awareness washes over my body at the thought of him watching the last few moments. A deeper warmth pulsed between my legs at the thought of him as one of the performers.

I know before Marcus speaks that he has returned. The scent of sandalwood reaches my nose in a heady introduction.

"In a coin toss, you always pick heads." His statement catches me off guard. I almost ask him to say it again but remember the kiss of leather waiting for my slip of the tongue.

It was an odd question when he asked it earlier. Now I see the purpose. "Yes, master."

"Of course." Marcus traces the outline of the mask covering my eyes then follows the line of my jaw. Finally, he reaches the curve of my upper lip, the whisper soft caress igniting the gooseflesh on my upper body. I smell my own arousal on his fingers.

"With you, the mind leads and you follow, always rational." Marcus kisses me, the barest brush of his lips to mine. Then he devours. His tongue probes the cavern of my mouth, insistent, demanding. "Always in control. But the heart is unsatisfied. Isn't that so, Bree?"

He is right. I am in control but I've made my life empty. I avoid all semblance of connections to avoid the mistakes and traps of my past.

"Yes." A quick smack on my rump reminds me of my manners. Cream surges from my sheath. "Yes, Master," I amend. The words don't trip on my tongue this time.

Marcus weaves a tight circle around my naked body, always touching, always close. A heady fragrance lingers in the air...the scent of maleness and sex. His breathing rasps in my ears, his scent fills my nostrils. The heat of his body consumes me.

"You want something more."

When Marcus presses against me this time, the heat of his skin burns against mine. He's removed his clothing. Gooseflesh tingles to life, reaching out to be closer to him.

The muscles of his chest ripple against my shoulders, his body taut and energized. I lean into the contact despite myself. Deep within the core of my womanhood, the resolve of my inhibitions melt to liquid fire. A moan escapes my throat as the fire leaps upward to flick at my heart.

Softer hands cup my face, the thumbs pressing against my mouth until my lips open. The warm rush of breath kisses my chin. Cinnamon. Lily. Another pair of lips nuzzle my neck from behind, nipping at the hollow beneath my jawline. Someone else is behind me now, their body hard where hers is soft.

I lean my head toward the body in front and arch my backside against the second body molded to me from behind, the rigid tip of an erection branding the flesh above my waist. Instinct only fills in the face in my darkness.

"Do you want us, sweet Bree?" Dual voices, deep, throaty, fill each ear.

My sex liquefies along the walls of my canal and dampen my thighs but I can't give him that final measure. I will not beg again for the attention I crave, for the love I desire.

"Yes." Then I add because I know. "Yes, mistress."

Strong hands encircle my waist, long fingers splay against my belly, pointing to the smoldering embers of my sex waiting to be stoked. Overhead, metal clanks against metal and my arms begin to lower. Hands cup my mons and I lean forward as the tension in the chains ease.

"Will you trust that desire? Allow yourself to feel it?"

The words collide on my tongue but I push them out. "I trust you."

Another kiss of cinnamon whispers across my mouth. "It's not us you need to trust, Bree. That's what this weekend was about. It is not about trusting me and Jon."

Jon's voice fills caresses the hollow beneath my ear. "You chose us."

"You trusted us from the beginning." Her voice. Her voice reaches deeper, touches more, finds more. "You can trust what you want and more importantly, who you want it with."

"We will never take you anywhere you don't want to go."

"We will be by your side as long as you want us there."

"Who do you need to trust?"

Their voices wrap around me like a silk scarf. With my heart lodged in my throat and my body smoldering with unsatisfied desire, I whisper the easiest word I've ever said. "Myself."

The world lifts from my shoulders. The emptiness recedes and in its place is only warmth.

Lily holds my face between her hands and says against my lips, each word a kiss. "You are worthy of love. Do you believe me?"

I can only nod.

"Say it, Bree. Say it so you-" a kiss softer than any I'd imagined "-believe it."

The emotion burns behind my eyes and clogs my chest as I say, "I am worthy of love."

Jon. "You are free to choose and be chosen."

Lily. "And you can trust those choices."

The words are easier this time. "I am free." I swallow the doubt, the fear. "And I trust myself."

The realization is another weight off my shoulders, a vice released from my heart.

They continue to press me forward, widening my stance with the firm pressure of a knee. My nipples brush against cool leather. A couch perhaps. I brace my hands shoulder width apart.

The broad span of Jon's chest blankets my back as his left hand parts the cleft in my cheeks. He teases the pucker of my anus with the tip of his cock while his right hand slips between the folds of my wet pussy. I gasp as the dual sensation steals the breath from my lungs.

"Then ask for what you want, Bree." Lily's voice is a caress in my ear. "It's not the same as begging when those you're asking truly love you."

With those single words the meaning becomes clear. I had begged for love from people who neither could nor would give it. But still I begged. If I were to only ask, Jon and Lily would fulfil my desire and chase away the emptiness within my body and soul. Asking is not the same as begging.

The mask still covers my eyes but it no longer matters. I do not need to see. I only need to feel. I exist only for the moment I will be filled completely.

"I want you, Jon. I want you, Lily. Can I have you? Please."

I don't have to wait long, either. Lily's kiss claims my mouth, her fingers in my hair a touchpoint and foundation for my connection. I feel her on every level, with every cell.

In the space of a heartbeat, the rasp of tearing cellophane punctuates the silence in the room. The taut shaft of a cock slips into the folds of my sex, lubricating it in my own desire. Slim fingers massage the swollen skin gently then slide further down and press my labia around the sliding penis. Familiar lips suckle at my breasts, the combination of sensations stoking each other like fuel to the fire.

My breath pauses as Jon withdraws then plunges in again. Soft words, incomprehensible except to my fluttering heart, brushes against my ear. Lips grazes my shoulder, kissing away the tension tightening my muscles.

A tight heat coils around my insides, flaring in the pit of my stomach. Each powerful thrust deepens his penetration and lifts me from the floor. My thoughts narrow as if down a dark tunnel, the only light the point of joining between my body and theirs. Sweat dampens my body.

Lily's mouth kisses my stomach, my breasts, licks a line up my throat until the heat of her breath scorches my cheek.

Jon thrusts deeply and pauses as my pussy clutches tightly around his thick shaft. I hear him moan softly and I'd long to see that pleasure reflected in his face if I wasn't about to implode.

"Lily," I whisper breathlessly. "Let me see you. Let me see you and Jon."

The ties holding the blindfold are released and I find Lily poised in front of me, her lips swollen with my kisses, her face reflecting the love filling my own heart. Jon's arms encircle my neck and shoulders, drawing me back against him, our bodies still intimately connected. I look over my shoulder into his eyes and see love again.

Whatever pain has filled my past drowns beneath the promise of the future. I will no longer be controlled by it. I am in charge.

I reach up and cup Jon's cheek with one hand, and Lily's

with the other. The connection between the three of us surge through me. I am complete again.

Only soft light chases away the darkness around us, a thousand flickering suns to glisten on the sheen of our sex dampened bodies.

"I don't want to ruin the moment," Jon said, his voice shaky and edged with lust. "But I need to finish fucking this woman into oblivion or my dick is going to fall off." He thrusts forward with his very hard cock to drive home the point.

Lily's eyes widen, and her mouth opens in a cute little "o" of surprise. I lean forward and plant a kiss on those very kissable lips.

"Good idea," I agree against her mouth. "Because if I don't come very soon I'm going to lose my mind."

Lily shrugs, smiles broadly and drops back against the sofa cushions. "Fuck away." She spreads her legs and finds her clit with two fingers. "I'll just enjoy from here."

The sight ramps my own desire even higher, something Jon obviously feels as he groans in sweet agony as my pussy tightens even further.

I grab her ankles and pull her forward. "That's too far away."

I flick my tongue across her fingers where they wait on her clit, push them aside and tease the swollen nub. I kiss the intimate flesh, feel the warmth of her body respond.

Jon's arms circle my waist as his hips press between my outstretched thighs, pushing them further apart. With a single thrust he plunges deeper into my canal, touching the center of my womanhood.

I gasp at the intrusion and look up, seeing Lily's sable eyes search mine and in the ebon depths I see my own passion and desire reflected.

Home. The word bounces around my head, and I find it belongs. However it has happened this quickly, they are my home. My center. A safe foundation to focus my love.

Behind me, Jon begins to rebuild the ache within me and I arch my hips backward and match his rhythm. His fingers bite into my buttocks, kneading my cheeks as he drives deeper until I think I will be swept away by the churning passion.

His movements quicken and I feel the change in his cock, the slight upturn of the head as it grazes the back wall of my canal on each thrust.

Stars dance in my vision but it's the electricity skittering across my flesh that steals my breath.

"Ask me, Bree," Lily prods, guiding my face until our eyes meet again.

There's no hesitation in my words. "Please, Lily. May I come?"

"Yes."

The wave crashes down and I cry out as the orgasm shatters through me. Jon pulls me into the next lunge of his body and his hips lift me from the floor. His body snaps back and he groans like a man dying a sweet death.

Deep within my sheath the ripple of his orgasm pumps down his cock and I clench tightly around the pulsing organ, drawing out his pleasure and finding the last blissful moments of my own.

We collapse against the sofa, breathless, drained of all strength, our bodies still intimate. Lily joins us, twining her body with ours.

In my mind I cannot separate our limbs. Where I leave off, they begin. I know, even in the hazy depths of my clouded mind, that this is not just love. It is something more. And I need it as much as I need my next breath.

Lily curls around us, pushing back the damp tendrils of hair from my face. She presses a tender kiss to my temple.

"Welcome home, my love."

Coolness envelopes our bodies as a blanket is drawn up around us.

I lay my head on Lily's chest, her heart fluttering in one ear while Jon's fills the other and slows from its wild race. Mine falls into sync with the two.

Right where it should be.

THE END

THANK YOU FOR READING

Reviews are the lifeblood of an author. Please consider leaving a review on any of your favorite review sites.

If you enjoyed Mastered by Degrees: The Collection, join Selena's newsletter for information on future additions to the *Six Degrees of Seduction* collection.

ABOUT THE AUTHOR

Selena Powers is an award-winning author of contemporary romance and erotic fiction. She fell in love with romance before she knew what it was, stealing paperback novels from her grandmother's closet when her mother wasn't looking.

She started writing naughty stories in high school, much to the pleasure of her classmates and the dismay of her principal.

She loves to travel and tells people that anything and everything they do could end up in her next novel, so if you recognize yourself in the pages of her books, remember you were warned.

Selena currently balances her life between the right brain and left brain, quality consultant and technical writer by day, romance writer by night.

Visit Selena Powers' Website

Visit Selena's website for more information, or subscribe to the newsletter for release day information, prizes, and more! Follow Selena on social media: @writerselenap on Twitter and @authors_maggie_and_selena on Instagram.

MORE FROM THE AUTHOR

Read *The Beast and the Barkeep* in a charity anthology benefitting
The Trevor Project:

Read The Beast and the Barkeep

www.ingramcontent.com/pod-product-compliance
Lightning Source LLC
Chambersburg PA
CBHW020317200626
46814CB00006BA/2295